BROKEN ROAD

LIMELIGHT SERIES BOOK #1

NEW YORK TIMES AND USA TODAY BESTSELLING AUTHOR

PIPER DAVENPORT

WITH USA TODAY BESTSELLING AUTHOR

JACK DAVENPORT

Sale of this book without a front cover may be unauthorized. If this book is coverless, it may have been reported to the publisher as "unsold or destroyed" and neither the author nor the publisher may have received payment for it.

Broken Road is a work of fiction. Names, characters, places, and incidents are the products of the author's imagination and are used fictitiously. Any resemblance to actual events, locales, or persons, living or dead, is entirely coincidental.

Cover Art
Jack Davenport

ROSES
FOR
ANNA

Thanks to my ever-faithful critique ladies, Liz Kelly, Anna Brooks, Sarah Smith, and Kim Gill.

You are amazing and we couldn't have done this without you!

All it took was one page and I was immediately hooked on Piper Davenport's writing. Her books contain 100% Alpha and the perfect amount of angst to keep me reading until the wee hours of the morning. I absolutely love each and every one of her fabulous stories. ~ Anna Brooks – Contemporary Romance Author

Get ready to fall head over heels! I fell in love with every single page and spent the last few wishing the book would never end! ~ Harper Sloan, NY Times & USA Today Bestselling Author

Piper Davenport just reached deep into my heart and gave me every warm and fuzzy possible. ~ Geri Glenn, Author of the Kings of Korruption MC Series

For Scott & Jess

*You two helped inspire this book and we're so glad you're
our forever friends.
Love you guys!*

Bam

I WAS IN hell. It was partially a hell of my own making… however, recognizing this didn't make my current predicament any easier.

The muffled sounds of the customary "end of tour debauchery" thumped through the wall behind me, but I wasn't quite done working yet. Our final show of the tour wasn't until tomorrow night, but the band was celebrating early. It sounded like the makings of another in a long line of notorious bashes being thrown by the "Reigning Crown Princes of Southern Rock," or whatever the press had labeled us this week.

Hadley, our manager's saintly assistant, had worked

out an arrangement with the theater to give us access to the large rehearsal room, currently being used as our own personal night club, and a small dressing room that had been set up for my scheduled interview. My eyes scanned my temporary prison, which had been furnished with two folding chairs, a small glass table, and a craft services cart containing bottled water, beer, and a basic deli platter.

Rainbow meat.

Sitting on a round, plastic platter was a familiar variety of sliced bread, bright orange triangular cheese slices, and what we not-so-affectionately called "rainbow meat." This culinary abomination earned its name due to the fact that it took on an iridescent hue after sitting out in the open for too long. I related to the sad contents of the platter. I, too, was a piece of meat that had been out too long. Everyone in the business knew to stay away from the rainbow meat. Everyone that is, except Sheila Roberts; SPIN magazine's writer of the year, notorious star fucker, and the very last person on earth I wanted to talk to. She was a tall bottle-blonde with the best tits her expense account would cover.

"Hi, Bam." Sheila's voice dripped with fake sincerity. "Thanks so much for meeting with me. I hear the tour has been amaaaahzing!"

I instantly disliked this woman. I should have been excited that SPIN wanted to do such a big piece on Roses for Anna, and that they had sent their 'hottest' reporter. I should have been excited that our first headlining tour had been sold out in almost every venue we played. I should have been happy about the success of last two singles. And I most *definitely* should have been excited the final show of the tour was tomorrow night… but I wasn't. I was fried.

"No problem, happy to finally get to sit down with you," I lied. I knew why she was here and what she *really* wanted to talk about.

Lately, the main goal of the press was to dig for information regarding my relationship with Melody Morgan, the reigning "Queen of Pop." When I was told that SPIN wanted to do this interview with only me, without the band, I agreed, but only under one condition: *"Absolutely no fucking questions about Melody."*

Those were the exact words I'd spoken to our manager when Chas informed me this interview was going to happen. He assured me that 'Sexy Sheila' would only be allowed to ask questions about the tour, the new album, and general band history. I didn't fully trust him, and the band was pissed at me for doing the interview alone, but what could I do? This is what the label wanted, so this is what management wanted.

"Let's jump right in, I'm sure you're dying to get back to your party," Sheila said.

That actually couldn't have been further from the truth. The last thing I wanted was to be trapped in a room full of phonics and money men. God knows I could blow off some steam, and I'd sure as hell earned it. But how? Get drunk, bang a groupie, get into a fight? The truth was, I was bored and tired of all of it, and for the first time I was trying to put all that shit behind me and *keep my cool.*

"Take your time, Miss Roberts. Can I get you anything? A drink perhaps?" I offered.

"Um no, I…I'm fine, thanks." Sheila studied me with renewed interest. "I'm sorry, I expected more of a—"

"Bad boy?" I provided.

"Well, there's no shortage of stories regarding the exploits of Roses for Anna, but now that I'm face-to-face with the 'Notorious B.A.M.,' you seem a touch more gentleman than wild man."

"Yeah, we know how to kick up a little dust from time to time, but we were raised to say 'sir' and 'ma'am,' and to always offer a lady a drink," I said smiling slowly.

This was all true, but I also knew when to lay on the southern charm, and I hoped my politeness would keep Sheila within the proper bounds during our interview.

Sheila set her digital recorder on the small glass table between us and hit record. She took a deep breath, looked at me with a staged intensity, changed her tone to what I assumed was her best "fuck me" voice, and began, "Childhood friends rock their way from the Deep South to the top of the charts. How does it feel to be the heartthrob at the center of it all?"

I now hated this woman.

"I don't know about being the center of anything," I countered, shifting uncomfortably. "But yeah, Jimmy, Zeke and I have known each other since we were kids."

"In Alabama right?"

"Yes ma'am, Elwood Alabama to be exact." I poured on the southern accent and flashed her a sly grin. I didn't want to be here, but I knew how to play the game. "Jimmy and I have known each other since seventh grade."

"How did you meet?"

"Well…funny story, we met…sort of…rescuing another kid from getting the shit kicked out of him. He was a skinny little runt with thick glasses, and some eighth graders were doing their best from, shall we say 'liberating him from his lunch money.'"

Sheila laughed.

"Jimmy and I didn't know each other, or this kid, but we both saw what was going down from opposite sides of the cafeteria. We locked eyes, jumped in, pulled the bully off, and proceeded to teach him a lesson about picking on weaker people."

She cocked her head. "Wow, you sounded more like a gang than friends."

"We were worse," I admitted. "We were a *band*. Jimmy and I hit it off and bonded over music right away. We loved all the same bands, mostly from the 90's…especially RatHound. Jimmy wanted to play bass and sing like Rex Haddon and I wanted to play the drums just like Jack Henry. Hell, I wanted to *be* Jack Henry. I even started growing my hair like his. Jimmy thought that was cool so we started our first band. The skinny kid with the glasses became our first guitarist. He was a great player but he never could fight for shit."

"So, Edward isn't your original guitar player?"

"No, no, no," I said with a chuckle. "Edward is el numero tres. He's been with the band for almost a year now. He came in to help out with the guitar tracks on the last album and ended up sticking around. He's great, but to be honest with you I think he'd rather be somewhere quiet with a glass of scotch and a big ol' book about art or something."

Sheila smiled. "When did you guys meet Zeke?"

"Junior year of high school—not that we were going to school much at this point. I've always loved to read, but never cared much for getting up early." Surprisingly, I started to drop my guard a little. "We were at a backyard party and Zeke was singing for another band. Jimmy was reaching his vocal limits and really wanted to concentrate on his bass playing. We saw Zeke's band play and, truth be told, we didn't like him much, but he had a PA system and a lot of confidence. He also said he could get us fake IDs, so naturally he was in the band."

"Was Zeke already a great singer back then?"

"Zeke?" I laughed. "He didn't *sing* so much as he… drunkenly yelled, with a lot of enthusiasm. He got good pretty quick, though…once he figured out the girls paid more attention to him when he actually sang well."

I started to relax a little more. Maybe I had been too hard on Sheila. Maybe she really was here to talk about the band and not all the recent TMZ bullshit. Maybe SPIN magazine wasn't interested in digging for dirt.

She continued, "Growing up in small town Alabama, did you ever think you'd end up writing hit singles, selling out shows across the country, and dating pop stars?"

And here she goes pulling out her shovel.

"Um, yeah…I guess we had pretty big dreams

right way…but uh…" I stumbled on my words. She had shifted the weight of the conversation just enough to trip me up. "We're really happy to have gotten here, together." I tried to recover and hoped the interview wasn't going in the direction I'd feared.

"That's great," she said, flatly.

I got the impression this wasn't the answer she was looking for. She more than likely wanted me to take all the credit for writing our last two singles and successfully spearheading our first tour as a headlining act. I could see her mentally shifting gears before she started the next line of questioning.

"So it's been a few months since your very public split with Melody Morgan, how are you doing?" she asked with obvious fake concern.

I stiffened.

"I'm doing great. Everything is cool. Thanks," I responded, as dryly as possible, hoping she would hop off this trail as fast as she hopped on.

"Given the high level of her celebrity status, was it tough for you to be romantically attached to the current 'queen of pop,' or was the additional publicity good for you and the band?"

"Um, well, neither. I try my best to keep my personal life and band life separate, ya know?" I once again tried to politely steer her back on course, but I was quickly losing my patience.

"Have you spoken to Melody lately and is it hard for you to hear your hit duet on the radio playing every hour, on the hour?"

"Well, I don't really listen to the radio, and we've been really busy working on our new album, and the tour—"

"It's just that it seemed like the whole world was really rooting for pop star and the rocker to make it the distance, and you seemed so in love," she continued.

Sonofabitch! This woman is relentless!

It was obvious she wasn't going to let this go and had no intention of talking about the band, our music, or our album…she really only wanted dirt. Gossip has become the biggest money maker in the entertainment industry, and this so called "journalist" wanted to make a name for herself through the flaming wreckage of my last relationship.

"Well, like I said, I don't talk about my private life, and have been focusing on our new album and this tour, so maybe we could just talk about that." I was now officially done being polite. I had been very clear with Chas about not answering questions about Melody and I couldn't believe the nerve of this so-called-journalist.

"Yes, of course! I absolutely want to talk about the new album, let's do that," she continued. "Did your recent breakup influence your songwriting on the new album?"

As soon as the words were out of her mouth, I was on my feet. I was ready to tell her that the interview was officially over, and that she could kiss my ass, but at that very moment, Jimmy came bounding through the door.

"Hey Baaaaaam, you're missing the party, maaaaaan!" Jimmy yelled through his ear to ear grin. Each of his hands contained an empty beer bottle, held high above his head. He was clearly wasted, which was nothing new these days.

"Come join the festivities, brother!"

I seized this opportunity to make my exit.

"You know what, Sheila? Jimmy's right, I really should get back to the party. Thanks for your time, we'll have to do this again sometime really soon." Before Sheila could manage to get another word out of her shocked face, I had grabbed Jimmy by the arm and exited the room.

"Hey man, what the hell!" Jimmy protested.

I pushed through the double doors leading into our party suite. I deposited Jimmy on the nearest couch, between two of our road crew, relieving him of his two empty bottles, and grabbing a fresh longneck from a nearby bar tray.

"Well, that's more like it," Jimmy said and took a pull from the bottle.

I scanned the sea of faces and red plastic cups for Chas Chambers, the band's manager, the architect of the SPIN interview and the current object of my full wrath. At 6' 8", Chas was easy to pick out of a crowd. He was a massive man, who had been a champion bare knuckle boxer in his native Manchester, England, before going into the business of band management. His fighting background had served him well in the business and as much as I couldn't stand him, I couldn't argue that he got things done. Zeke had insisted that we hire him as the band's manager two years ago. Until then, I had managed the band, but Zeke felt like this gave me "too much power" and so made an ultimatum; hire Chas, or Zeke would quit.

I should have let Zeke fuckin' quit.

Chapter Two

Lucy

I WIPED MY sweaty palms over the waist of my little black dress and took a deep breath. I couldn't believe my parents were making me *do* this now. I mean, I could… this was my *job*, but I would have preferred a quiet, private meeting, over a conversation directly following a show… which I'd missed. I couldn't even tell the band what I thought of their performance, which was important when trying to convince them to do something for you.

"Talk to Roses for Anna about opening up the tour," Dad said.

"Me?"

"Yeah, baby, you."

"No problem," I'd said, but internally I'd sighed. I didn't argue. This was part of my job description after all, and it was a job I loved. I was good at it. I'd been raised on the road, raised with some of the best (and worst) people in the world. Taught to survive on my wits, humor, and talent. I had this.

But it was Bam Bam freaking Nelson. If there was a sexier man on earth, I'd be hard-pressed to name one, and now I was going to have to have a conversation with him. Would I be able to resist his "Yes, ma'am, thank you, ma'am, let me remove your panties with my teeth, ma'am" charm? Not that he was offering, but what if he did offer? I sighed. *God*! I paused my walk down the long hallway to squeeze my legs together. He checked every sex box on the planet (including mine if I was lucky).

But then on top of all that, my dad actually had the nerve to warn me about him. As if I didn't know about his reputation or didn't have the good sense to stay away from musicians. But this was Bam Nelson, so perhaps he did have a point.

I shook away my thoughts. I had to focus.

Pushing the door open to the party room, I scanned the area and my heart dropped. No Bam. Damn. I'd have to talk to Chas. I hated Chas. Chas was a douche. As in, CEO of Massengill…and he was handsy to boot.

I shuddered, but forced my feet to move toward the band's manager.

"Lucy!" he greeted, his large hand waving me forward. "You're a sight for sore eyes, love."

I forced a smile and stopped far enough away so

he couldn't touch me. "Hey, Chas. I'm looking for Bam. Is he around?"

Chas sidled closer. "He's in an interview right now."

"Do you know when—?"

"Keep that bitch away from me, Chas!"

I jumped at the angry voice and turned toward it. Bam stood in the doorway; looking as though he was ready to murder Chas. Which might not be the *worst* thing.

* * *

Bam

I finally spotted Chas and began pushing my way through the swell of partygoers. He was standing at the back of the room, in a roped off area reserved for VIP guests, speaking with a curvy redhead woman who had her back to me. I couldn't see her face, but immediately knew she wasn't with our crew. Chas was wearing his "money face," which was reserved for only making deals.

"Keep that bitch away from me, Chas!" I shouted over the earsplitting music.

The woman spun to face me and I lost my mind for a second. Fuck, she was gorgeous.

"What bitch?" Chas demanded, his sleazy salesman smile dropping from his face, and pulling my focus back to him. "Where's Sheila, and why aren't you at the bloody interview?" Chas' gruff, Northern English accent was in full effect.

"The interview is *over* and there won't be another one," I snapped back.

"What do you mean, *over*?" he demanded. "You've only been in there for ten fucking minutes!"

"Excuse me, Mr. Nelson," the redhead said in a clear attempt to interrupt the tornado of testosterone she'd currently found herself in the middle of.

I ignored her and continued my tirade.

"She started in with all that Melody gossip crap and I told you I wasn't gonna talk about her! Sheila didn't give a shit about the band or the new album. She probably hasn't even listened to it! She clearly wanted to get her shovel full of dirt!"

"Mr. Nelson, if I could just—" the redhead continued, this time with enough intensity to pull my attention away from Chas.

As she spoke, my anger dissipated. She was stunning. She was around 5'4" but seemed to float a few extra inches off the ground. Her deep red hair fell in soft waves well below her bare shoulders. She wore a skintight, but otherwise fairly conservative black cocktail dress. She was dressed for business, but still fully showing off all of her amazing curves. I could see why she had Chas' full attention.

"Excuse me," I interrupted. "I need to speak with my manager." I knew I was being an asshole, and this woman was hot, but after months of trying to keep my cool, Sheila had sent me over the edge. "The interview is done," I snapped, my full attention back on Chas.

"Done my ass, mate." Chas took a deep breath. "Now, I'll go smooth things over with Sheila, you take a minute to get your shit together, have a drink, or do whatever the fuck you need to do, and we'll start the interview over."

"No way, *mate*. This band has worked too hard over the last ten years to be reduced to this tabloid bullshit! I'm not doing it!"

"Well, *mate*," Chas said before taking a carefully calculated pause, "Maybe you should have thought of that before fucking that little pop tart of yours in front of the whole bleedin' world."

Before I could think, I swung. This was not a smart move on my part, for several reasons. For starters, it's a little hard to play the drums with a broken hand, and had I connected with the side of beef, otherwise known as Chas' face, I certainly would have done so. Secondly, starting a fistfight with management is typically frowned upon, even in our crazy line of work. Lastly, and perhaps most importantly, there was Chas' impressive underground boxing record. It was likely his great skill level that allowed him to so easily slip my punch. He was quick for such a massive man, and even though he looked shocked that I had swung at him, he calmly stepped to the side, causing me to momentarily lose my balance.

"What the fuck are you on about?" Chas shouted.

I briefly made eye contact with the stunning woman, and just as before, I felt my burning anger start to cool, but I was too wound up to fully control myself.

Chas, now looking somewhat amused, began to goad me, "It's a good thing you swat them drums better than you fight," he said laughing.

He wasn't laughing for long.

My next punch, a left uppercut to the kidney, didn't miss. At a little over six-feet tall, I didn't have any kind of advantage on my opponent, but after nearly fifteen years of drumming, my left had some power that he wasn't expecting, and he felt it.

By now, the entire room had turned their attention to the two raging idiots in the back of the room. The DJ had killed the music and the party goers had begun pulling out their cell phones, no doubt in order to film the fray.

Chas winced in pain and staggered back, stunned from the body blow. Perhaps more stunned that I had actually hit him. But then he looked at me, stood straight up, and I knew I was in trouble. He hit me so hard I was out before I hit the floor.

As I came to, I could see the beautiful redhead with a mixture of horror, concern, and disgust on her face looking down on me. I then saw Chas enter my blurry frame of vision.

"You need to get your head right before I knock it clean off…and, by the way," he continued, leaning inches away from my face. "This is Lucy Haddon." His hushed tone was controlled, but somehow more venomous than usual. "She's here to talk with us about the possibility of playing the opening slot on a RatHound reunion tour."

Shit.

I blacked out.

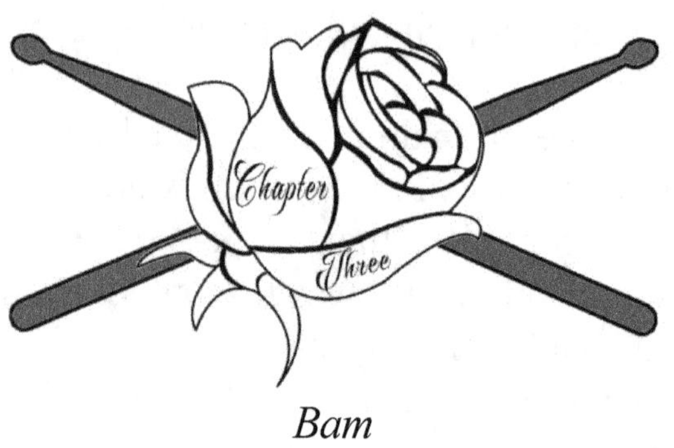

Bam

MY JOB IS supposed to be easy. I'm the drummer. I hit things. I typically stick to drums, cymbals, and the occasional cowbell, however, the last thing I remember hitting was our manager. Things were very cloudy after that. My head was spinning and my ears were ringing louder than they ever had in my life. This, of course, was saying something given that my chosen profession often leaves me ear level with Marshall stacks and floor monitor speakers cranked to ten. Through my blurred vision, I could see my manager and the mystery redhead hovering over me. Chas was clearly pissed, but what was he saying?

I struggled to make sense of the all the words

coming out of his mouth, but managed to make out two things very clearly over the ear-splitting din… "RatHound" and "world tour."

Shit.

As soon as the words registered, I understood exactly what was going on…who the mystery redhead was and how colossally bad I had screwed up. The woman I had just humiliated myself in front of was Lucy Haddon, daughter of Rex Haddon, lead singer and bassist of RatHound. Lucy had recently been made the band's new manager after the recent announcement of their long awaited reformation.

I sprang to my feet as quickly as I could, and a wave of nausea hit me.

Don't throw up, dumbass. That's the last thing you need.

I extended my right hand to Lucy, which ended up six inches to the left off the mark.

"Hey there…uh…pleased to meet you, you're Bam," I stammered.

She blinked slowly.

"No wait," I continued, trying to recover. "I'm *me, and you're* Bam."

Before I could clear my head, she turned on her heels and started to walk, with great purpose, out of the room.

"Wait!" I called.

I took one step forward and my feet instantly gave out from under me. Chas had clearly not pulled back on his punch, and I was likely concussed. It wasn't the first time and I was already dreading the headache I was going to have in the morning.

"I thought your guys were ready, Chas. Thanks for wasting our time," Lucy called out over her shoulder without looking back.

"What the *fuck* was that all about!" Zeke bellowed as he charged toward me. "Like we need *more* of this viral video shit from you!"

"Back off him, Zeke!" Jimmy shouted, and threw himself between the two of us.

Zeke shoved Jimmy. "Fuck you, man, stop protecting him!"

"He's already hurt, you asshole, just back off!"

By now the crowd around us was swelling with people pouring into the suite from all around the backstage area. Including Sexy Sheila. She pushed her way through the crowd, pulled out her phone and, click. She flashed me a quick smile, and was gone.

I could see the cover of SPIN now. A picture of me on the floor, with my left eye swelled like a cantaloupe, half my band on top of me with the headline: "Maniac redneck drummer storms out of interview and attacks manager in front of rock icon's daughter."

"Lucy! Miss Haddon!" I shouted, trying again to scramble to my feet.

I had gotten used to the band being pissed off at me lately, but this was different. I knew I deserved their wrath, and I felt lower than I ever had in my life. RatHound were our heroes. This was the band that made me want to play music for the first time.

"I'm sorry, guys. I didn't know who she was. How was I supposed to know?" I pulled myself up, my feet shaky.

I steadied my stance and started for the door, pushing my way through the mass of people. Security had already begun removing people from the building and collecting as many cell phones and cameras as they could. It was no use, the story, and likely video of the fight would hit the internet within hours.

I continued to push my way through the hallway, desperately searching for Lucy. I had to find her. I had to somehow explain myself. I could feel the left side of my face getting hotter as the knot above my eye continued to swell. I checked for blood above my eye, but felt nothing.

At least he didn't cut me.

"Lucy! Lucy! Miss Haddon!" I shouted unsuccessfully. Either she couldn't hear me, or she was ignoring my pathetic howls…I was guessing the latter. She couldn't have gotten too far, but the busy backstage area of the theater and the double vision were not making my situation easier.

Having covered most of the theater's backstage and lobby, I decided to look outside. I found a side door, pushed through it and was met with a cold blast of February air. It felt good on my burning face, but being dressed in only jeans and a t-shirt, stung almost everywhere else. I was ill-equipped for the Washington weather. I ran around to the front of the theater just in time to see Lucy walking down the steps in front of the box office.

"Lucy! Miss Haddon! Stop!" Fuck. I couldn't see straight and grabbed my head and I walked toward her. "It's me Bam Nelson! Please let me explain!"

Lucy continued her quick stride, her kitten heels angrily tapping out a steady cadence. She was now dressed in a bright red wool pea-coat and a white scarf. Her red hair flowed out from underneath a matching white beret. She looked amazing.

"Miss Haddon…Lucy…damn it, woman, stop!" I shouted as a grabbed her shoulders and spun her around.

She faced me with fire burning in her deep brown eyes. "Get your hands off me!" she demanded, and continued her stride.

"Just give me second to explain!"

"I've given you far more than a second, Mr. Nelson. I came here tonight to personally extend an invitation for you to join us this summer. I was told that you were on the rise and had your act together. Clearly, I was given bad information."

She was beautiful beyond words. So beautiful in fact, it was hard to look at her for too long. For some reason, in that moment, I didn't care about letting the band down or fighting with Chas or TMZ. I only saw the look of disappointment on her face, and I knew I never wanted to see that look again.

"Bam," I bit out. "Please call me Bam."

"*Mr. Nelson*, please get out of my way so I can deliver the bad news to my father. I need to let him know we have to find a new opening act." Her voice took on a breathy quality to it and she raised her nose slightly, which gave her a regal air.

"Please, don't do that." I let out a frustrated sigh. "You have no idea what RatHound's music means to me. Give me a chance to show you that. What happened back there is not who I am, not who we are as a band." I tried to sound like my normal confident self, but this woman made me feel very exposed. I couldn't figure out why I cared so much about what this complete stranger thought of me. It wasn't just about the gig. I actually cared about what she must have been thinking of me. Chas was way out of line about what he said about me and Melody, but I still shouldn't have swung at him. I lost control, and that's something I was trying really hard *not* to do. "We'd love to do the tour. We're ready. I assure you we're ready," I stressed.

Lucy studied me for a few, tense seconds. "You should know, my parents saw you at the Gunnach Pharmaceuticals Christmas charity concert and said you "blew them away" after only two songs. They knew right then you were the right band to be the support act for the entire summer tour of the US. I was inclined to believe them, but after what I saw back there, there is no way in hell I'm bringing that kind of drama into my father's world."

RatHound's issues with drugs and alcohol in the past were legendary, so I was well aware of her concerns. I took a deep breath and focused on using my charm. "Look. What you saw back there was the perfect storm of a lot of things coming to a head. But I can fix this. I just have a few things going on."

"Yes, I'm aware of those "things," Mr. Nelson, the whole world is aware," she said sarcastically.

My flesh crawled. Last summer, several minutes of video footage of Melody and I fucking like rabbits made its way to the internet. We'd made it together intending to delete it later, but the video went viral quickly and brought a lot of unwanted attention on me and the band. Melody was somewhat used to the attention, and it didn't really seem to bother her, but it bothered me, and it sure as hell bothered the band.

I tried to change the subject. "Please call me Bam. Mr. Nelson sounds like you're talking to my dad or something."

"Mr. Nelson," she said in what I sensed was her driest "professional" voice. "Let me be very clear." She paused, for what looked like dramatic effect, and straightened her coat. "Roses for Anna will *not* be opening for RatHound this summer or on *any* other subsequent tours. Good evening."

Good evening? Who was this adorable woman?

She reminded me of a little girl playing dress up in her mother's coat, pretending to be in the topsy-turvy world or Rock and Roll world of SHOW BUSINESS. But this was no little girl. I couldn't believe how beautiful she was. Her skin was pale and lightly freckled and her brown eyes were bright and intense. She was sweet looking, but sexy as hell.

"I understand why you'd say that, I really do. I'd probably feel the same way. But if you give me one more chance to make a first impression, you won't be sorry."

"That's not how life works. You don't get a do-over on first impressions. You screwed up and I'm out of here. Now please don't waste any more of my time."

"I get it." I crossed my arms and raised an eyebrow. "I'm an asshole. It's clear I can't change your opinion on that, but please don't punish the rest of the guys in my band just because I lost it tonight. For their sakes, please meet me for coffee tomorrow morning and hear me out. If you still hate my guts, I promise I'll leave you alone."

She paused, and I could see the faintest smile begin to creep up on the right side of her mouth, which she quickly stowed away before speaking again.

"Nine a.m. at the coffee place next to the theater. I'll give you twenty minutes. Don't be late…*Mr. Nelson.*"

She walked away and left me standing alone feeling puzzled by what had just happened…and very turned on. With my half frozen body and my throbbing head, I made my way up the stairs, back toward the side entrance. I needed ice for my head and a drink for everything else.

What was I doing? I couldn't think about Lucy Haddon right now. I shouldn't have been thinking about *any* woman right now, let alone the daughter of the guy who I essentially wanted to work for this summer, and whose band's music changed my life. I had to get back to the band and Chas right away and let them know about the coffee meeting rescue mission I had set up for the following morning.

I reached the side door and began pounding out a steady, familiar rhythm. Years ago, when we were playing crappy nightclubs, it was a common occurrence for a band member to get locked out of the venue during load in or a smoke break. We'd devised a kind of "secret knock" that we could all bang out in case of such emergencies. It's pretty amazing how good we all got at hearing that particular knock over all manner of noise.

After a few minutes of my epic door solo, I began to shout. I was freezing in my jeans and t-shirt, and my fingers and toes where completely numb.

"Hey! Let me in! I'm with the band!"

Thump…thump…thump.

"It's Bam with Roses for Anna, let me the fuck in!" I yelled louder.

Thump...thump.

A few moments later I heard a muffled, yet familiar voice on the other side of the thick metal door.

"Bam? 'Zat you?" a raspy voice called out.

"Winston? Winston, hey man let me in!"

The door swung open and the man who had been on the road with us since the very early age of the band, stood before me wearing his trademark ratty bell-bottom jeans, red flannel shirt, and an ear to ear grin.

"What the fuck you doin' out there, brother?" he asked jovially, as he stood aside.

"Trying to change a woman's mind." I scurried in, welcoming the overheated air of the backstage area.

"Shit, brother, that's dangerous work. How'd it go?"

"Well, I've only got the one black eye, so there's that. Where's the band?" I asked, as I started walking toward the party suite.

"We're almost packed up." Winston's pace quickened in order to match mine.

"Chas got the band on the bus right after whatever the fuck that was that went on earlier. We didn't know where you were. Chas is flipping out."

"It's okay. I'll take care of him."

Winston was the only member of our road crew that had been there from the beginning. He saw our very first bar show and said we "had something." Until then, we were too young to play twenty-one and over venues, so we rehearsed a lot and only played the occasional all-ages show. We didn't have much stage experience, but we were tight, and took the music very seriously. Winston was a retired roadie who had toured with The Black Crowes throughout the 90s. He said he saw something special in us, but that we were "green as a frog's bare ass." He became our Obi Wan Kenobi, and our most loyal friend.

"I hate that limey prick," Winston said, his raspy voice barely pushing through his thick whiskers. "I heard you hit him? 'Zat true?"

"Yeah, but I shouldn't have. I lost my cool."

"Well, good for you anyway. Things haven't been as fun since he came on board…until tonight that is."

I could clearly hear in his voice that Winston was smiling from underneath his scraggly mess of a dirty blonde beard that covered most of his face.

We reached the loading dock and could see the band van, and Chas' car pulling away.

I ran up to the van and banged on its side right as it started to accelerate.

The van screeched to a halt, followed by Chas' black Bentley. Chas flew out of his car, followed quickly by Zeke and then Jimmy. Edward stayed in the van. I *knew* the new guy was smart.

"Where the fuck have you been?" Chas demanded.

"Before you say anything, I'm sorry and I'm going to fix this," I said.

"And how the hell are you planning on doing that, sunshine?" Chas growled.

"Lucy Haddon has agreed to meet with me. We're having coffee in the morning," I explained.

"What?" Zeke yelled. "You think we're going to let you meet with her *alone* after what you just pulled with Sheila tonight?"

"He's right," Chas said. "You aren't doing a thing, and you're not meeting with anyone. You're gonna get your ass in that van and pray that *I* can fix this."

Who the hell did Chas think he was? This was *my* band, not his. I took a deep breath and stowed my anger for the moment.

"I understand how you feel, Chas, but the meeting is set. I've smoothed things over for the moment and she's agreed to meet me for coffee, so that's exactly what I'm going to do. This is my band, and I don't need your permission."

"But you will need a straw for that coffee after I knock all your teeth out." Chas started toward me when Winston stepped in.

"Hey there brother Chas," he said in his signature slow, steady tone. "Let's hold on for one second."

"Stay the fuck out of this you dirty hippie," Chas snapped.

They were now standing chest to chest, Chas towering over Winston's straw-like frame. Winston may have been scrawny, but he'd been around the business as long as Chas and knew how to handle himself. He was also fiercely loyal to the band, hated Chas, and was certifiably insane.

"Sure thing, brother," he responded coolly. "I'm just gonna need you to go ahead and back away from my drummer first."

He took one step backward and slowly lifted the front of his "undershirt," a ratty 2012 European tour t-shirt, revealing a revolver tucked into his jeans waste band.

Just when I thought this night couldn't get more interesting.

Bam

AFTER A FEW moments of the standoff between Winston and Chas, I started to get a little nervous. This wasn't the first time I'd seen Winston pull his gun on someone. However, this was the first time I'd seen him do so to someone in *our* camp. Bar owners that didn't want to pay the band, sure. Drunken, sexually frustrated frat boys that wanted to kick our asses, sure. This *was* the road after all, but this was new territory for our road manager. Apparently I wasn't the only one who'd been on the road too long.

"You pull a gun on me, you better use it." Chas' words were slow and cold.

"I ain't drawin', just showin' you, so you know I mean business," Winston replied.

"I'll shove that piece up your arse—"

"Back off, both of you," I warned as I stepped between them. The last thing we needed was Winston in jail or a hole in Chas silk suit.

"Don't you tell me what to do, boy. I've been doin' this job since before you discovered your dick," Chas said.

"I ain't 'fraid to go back to prison!" Winston shouted.

I bit back a laugh as I faced Winston. "I appreciate your enthusiasm, brother, but I think you can stand down now." I turned back to Chas. "Chas, I'm trying to fix this, just calm down and we can figure this out. I don't want to fight—I don't want any more trouble."

"Trouble? Trouble? All you bring us is trouble these days!" Zeke shouted. "Melody Morgan, Sheila Roberts, and now Lucy *fucking* Haddon! You fuckin' blew opening for RatHound... *RatHound*."

"I know, Zeke, and I'm telling you I'm going to fix this," I said.

"No, *we* are going to fix this," Zeke countered. "There's no way I'm letting you meet with her alone tomorrow. No way Chas is going to let you!"

"Let me?" I snapped back. "What do you mean 'let me?' This is *our* band Zeke. Yours, mine, Jimmy's, *our* band. And this sure as hell isn't Chas' band!"

"That's right Bam, it's *our* band not your damned solo act, so we're all going to meet with her tomorrow."

"Fine, Zeke." I threw my hands up. "We'll all go. One big happy fuckin' family."

The cracks in my band were widening. Zeke and Chas were clearly vying for control of the band. Jimmy had always had my back, but I could even feel him pulling away. He seemed to be becoming more and more isolated these days. Who even knew what Edward was thinking?

He had been the band's third guitarist since our formation, and even though he seemed eager to join us eight months ago, his interest already seemed to be waning. I couldn't understand why this rift was happening now when everything was going so great. The new album and single were doing well, and the tour was entirely sold out. Our *first* headlining theater tour and we were selling out. We should have been happy.

"We'll all go," I continued. "We'll talk, she'll see we're the right band for the tour, and everything will be okay."

"It'd better be Bam," Zeke said, his eyes locked on me.

Or what? I thought. It was moments like this that reminded me that I never *really* knew what Zeke thought of me. Not entirely.

The ride to the hotel in the band van was dead silent. Winston and the road crew always rode in their own separate van and Chas and his long-suffering assistant Hadley Simon traveled in Chas' prized

Bentley. We didn't even have a proper tour bus and that fat bastard drove around in a Bentley, *with a personal assistant.* I actually felt bad for Hadley. She seemed sweet and I couldn't figure out why she'd put up with Chas, or *us* for that matter. She was in her early thirties, cute as hell and spent most of her time fighting off the advances of sleazy rock promoters. She seemed a bit too smart to stick around all this bullshit for too long.

The band van was always reserved for only us— no fans, no business people, no girlfriends. This was our sacred space. Our place to write, our place to fight, and tonight it was our place to sit and stew in silence. Typically, we'd be laughing, talking about the night's show or listening to music. The drive after the show always served as a bonding time, but lately I felt more and more distant from the band.

Zeke's resentment of my recent high-profile relationship and the attention it brought on the band was growing. He hated that some people only knew of the band because of who I was, or more specifically, who I was dating.

To make matters worse, I had written a song for Melody before we broke up. Roses for Anna served as her backup band for the recording. Even though Melody was known as a pop singer, she was actually a great rock singer. She had asked me to write a song for her in order to showcase this other side of her. The song ended up on a very popular movie soundtrack. The movie and the song, billed as a duet between Melody Morgan with Roses for Anna, were huge hits. This should have been good news for the band, but not everyone saw it this way. Some members felt it softened our image.

Hadley checked us into the hotel and handed each of us our room keys. The sound of our roller bags on the hallway carpet was the only thing audible as we made our way to our rooms.

* * *

Lucy

What the hell am I doing?

I sat in the Town Car heading back to my apartment and verbally chastised myself. I was free. I had all the ammunition in the world to go back to my parents and let them know Roses for Anna would be a bad addition to the tour. But, no. What did I do? I fell for Bam and his southern charm, hook, line, and sinker. I was an idiot. A horny one. Which might be why I'd let him charm me.

I lowered the glass between me and my driver. "Sully?"

"Yes, Miss Haddon?"

"I need a burger, please."

"Of course, Miss Haddon."

"And a shake," I added. "And probably some onion rings."

He met my eyes in the rearview mirror. "Your usual?"

"Yes, please." I smiled. "Thanks, Sully."

"My pleasure."

Sullivan Wallace had been my bodyguard and driver since I was ten. He was kind of my best friend…to be honest, most days I felt like he was my only friend. He'd been hired by my parents when threats had been made against the family. Coincidentally, the threats started around about the same time Dad went into rehab. It was a shit time in my life and most days I wanted to forget it. My brother had his own driver, as did my parents. But Sully was all mine, and even after the threats had been eliminated, he'd stayed. He was my dad's age, unmarried, which was weird since he was gorgeous. Tall and muscular, his dark hair was peppered with white and he kept a slight beard that gave him a Pierce Brosnan look.

"Sully?"

"Yes, Miss Haddon?"

"Will you ever call me Lucy?"

"Probably not, Miss Haddon."

I wrinkled my nose. "I think that's ridiculous, Mr. Wallace."

He chuckled. "I'm aware, Miss Haddon."

We pulled up to the drive-thru and I ordered, then he drove around to the window and paid. He handed me my milkshake, but not the food. There were two rules for riding with Sully. No food or sex in his Town Car. The second rule was only verbalized when my first boyfriend and I made out in the back of the car when I was sixteen. He didn't last long and I was pretty sure Sully did something to scare him away, but I was never able to prove it, nor was I ever sure it was over protecting me or his car…he was weird about his car.

We arrived at my high-rise building and Sully walked me up to my apartment. "I'm not going out again tonight, Sully. You can take off for the evening."

"I'll see you tomorrow," he said.

"Thank you."

He smiled and took off, and I set my food on the counter, changed into yoga pants and a T-shirt, then dug into my food. Ohmigod, I loved a good burger. My butt wasn't much of a fan, but as I took another bite, I couldn't even give a modicum of shit about it.

I shoved an onion ring into my mouth just as a knock at my door came. I checked the peephole and pulled open the door. "Hi, Daddy."

"Hey, baby girl." He leaned down and kissed my cheek. "Hmm, onion rings. The meeting went that badly?"

Okay, I had a choice to make here. Knowing my dad, he already knew exactly what happened…but do I gloss over that and make my case as to why I'm letting Bam meet with me tomorrow?

"Come on in and I'll give you the low-down," I said.

My dad was one of the sexiest men alive, according to People Magazine's 1994 and 2001 editions. He was almost fifty-three years old, but still looked like he was in his thirties. Tall, dark-haired, blue eyed and one hell of a musician, he was a legend…and he was madly in love with my mother which was another reason women wanted him. Who wasn't attracted to a man who would never stray? Even with his drug and alcohol issues of the past, he never once cheated on my mother.

"Where's Mom?" I asked, and shoved another

onion ring in my mouth.

"Home."

"She's missing all the fun."

"She didn't miss anything." He grinned. "I wore her out."

I covered my ears. "Nope. No. Don't want to know. Gross, Dad."

He chuckled and grabbed a ring. "Fill me in."

"What did you hear?"

"Epic fight, Bam took Chas down…sort of. Possible concussion."

I gasped. "Bam has a concussion?"

"Luce. Focus. Bam's good."

I nodded. "Right."

I filled him in on the events of the evening, leaving nothing out except my attraction to the drummer. My dad did *not* need to be made aware of the reaction of my private parts when Bam Bam Nelson was around.

"Wow," Dad breathed out.

"Did I screw it up?"

"Why the hell would you think you screwed it up?"

"Because you don't need that kind of drama, Daddy. I should probably cancel the meeting tomorrow."

"Nope. You're taking that meeting."

"I am?"

"Baby girl, that's the band I want. I can handle drama; I've been married to your mother for over thirty years—"

I snorted out a laugh.

He smiled. "What I need to know is if Roses for Anna can handle a dry tour."

"I will find out tomorrow morning, then."

He cocked his head and studied me.

"What?"

He narrowed his eyes. "Do I need to warn you about him again?"

"What? No. Why? That's dumb, Dad." I focused on my shake and took a couple of sips in an effort not to nervously rant.

"Baby girl."

"Dad. I'm twenty-five years old, I'm running your tour, I'm an adult. You need to let me be one. I can handle Bam Bam Nelson. The man has the name of a cartoon caveman or cavebaby—what-ever."

He raised an eyebrow. "Do you think I've forgotten about the T-shirts and posters? You haven't been out of this house for that long."

"Dad, you were the one that asked me to meet with them, remember?"

"You're right, I'm sorry and I trust you." He smiled and threw his hands up in mock surrender.

"Good."

"Okay, I'm gonna get back to your mom. I'll talk to you tomorrow." He kissed me again and then headed out the door.

I finished my burger, grabbed a glass of wine, and flopped onto the sofa for a chick flick marathon, both excited and terrified to meet with Bam in the morning.

Bam

“**C**HICKS DIG SCARS.” That was all my dad said when I was eight years old and cut my right bicep open on a rusty nail sticking out from our back fence. The gash required four stitches and I was worried about being horribly disfigured for life. That was one of his better parenting moments.

I stood in front of the hotel room mirror. The giant purple wound above my left eye wouldn't leave a scar, but there was nothing I could imagine chicks digging about the current state my face. I looked like shit. To make matters worse, the headache express had arrived right on time, and just pulled into migraine station.

My phone buzzed. It was a text from Hadley: *Wheels up in five.*

I gently slid my sunglasses on, hoping to obscure my eye, and being extra careful not to provoke the angry volcano god currently residing on my face. Grabbing my bag, I headed down to the lobby.

"Hey," I quietly greeted the band who had all assembled, along with Chas, in the hotel lobby. Jimmy was texting on his phone, Edward was reading a book, and Zeke was laying flat on his back on the lobby couch with his hat over his eyes.

Chas was the only one who responded. "We have a few minutes before we have to leave so let's talk about the game plan for this meeting."

I nodded but was still pissed about the way Chas was suddenly telling me how things were going to be *in my band.*

"I'm gonna do the talking and you lot are gonna sit there and smile like good lads. And *you*"—Chas looked directly at me—"Not a fucking finger, mate."

I said nothing.

"I've worked too hard for you lot only to have you blow it when the big opportunities come knocking," Chas said in a low voice.

"What do you mean, *you've* worked hard?" I asked, my eyes meeting his. "This band has been busting its ass for years before we even knew your name."

"Look, mate, look at it however you want, but you don't know everything that goes on regarding the business matters of this band," Chas said.

"I sure as hell should!" I snapped back. "We *all* should!"

Zeke was laying still, his arms folded.

"Chas, did you know something about this RatHound tour beforehand?" I demanded.

Jimmy and Edward turned to stare at Chas now.

"What's your problem, Bam?" Zeke broke his silence and sat up suddenly. "Why don't you let Chas do his damn job? You're acting like this tour is a bad thing. Besides, you're the one who fucked this thing up for us. Let *him* deal with it. He's the band's manager, not you!"

Something didn't feel right. Zeke should have been just as pissed about this as I was. I understood him being angry at me about last night, but this was something different.

"Whatever. We'll talk about this later. We don't have time to get into this, we can't be late," I said.

We piled into the van and made our way to the coffee shop two doors down from the theater. Café le Cerf was about as old and historic as the theater itself. We arrived a few minutes early and Lucy was already there, sitting at a table for two, busily typing on her phone.

Damn, she was gorgeous. I instantly regretted not standing my ground and meeting her alone. For some reason I didn't want the ugly drama of my band to spill onto her. I didn't want her to see even a glimpse of the man I was last night. I didn't want to let her down.

There's that feeling again. Why do I care so much about what she thinks of me?

Lucy glanced up from her phone, looking momentarily surprised and I ventured a guess it was because the entire band and our manager were moving toward her.

"Hi there, love," Chas sang out, instantly laying on his schmoozing voice.

"Chas. Hello," she replied pleasantly. "I didn't realize the *whole band* would be here. I would have gotten a bigger table." She stared directly at me when she said this.

Shit. I knew it. It was just supposed to be the two of us.

"But that's great," she continued. "Since I didn't get the chance to meet everyone last night. How's your eye, Bam?" she asked me sweetly, but was clearly taking a dig at me.

"It's fine, thanks," I said sheepishly, pulling my sunglasses a little tighter to my face. "Again, I'm really sorry about last night."

Chas shot me a cold look.

"Mr. Nelson asked for another chance, so here we are. Let's just move on and see if we can talk business," Lucy said.

Chas forced his best attempt at a smile and I gave him a look that I'd hoped conveyed something along the lines of "eat a flaming bag of shit." We moved to a *slightly* larger table in the corner, and crowded around it as Lucy started, "As you may have heard, RatHound has recently reformed, and is playing a six week tour this summer across the United States. Until last night, we were very interested in having Roses for Anna open for the band for the entire tour."

"Well, we're here to talk," Chas said.

Lucy continued, ignoring him. "My father has seen you play and is sold on you guys. He feels like your band is the real deal and that's very important to him."

"It's important to us as well, and we're all huge RatHound fans," Zeke said, sounding a bit too eager for my taste.

Back off you fucking animals.

Chas cut in again, "Well, we'd love to play the dates and would be happy to start reviewing the offer with our lawyers."

"Let's not get too ahead of ourselves, gentlemen," she replied. "There's an important factor to consider, and after last night, I'm not convinced you're the right act for the bill."

"Did you see last night's show?" Zeke asked. "Did you see the crowd's response? Hear our music? We're the *perfect* band for the bill!"

"I haven't personally seen you play live yet, but honestly, my concerns are not about your music, or the popularity of the band," she explained. "You guys are solid in those departments. I'm more concerned about the chaos factor." She looked at me again. "Drugs and alcohol tore RatHound apart. The band members have each cleaned up over the years, and their shared sobriety has been the main reason they've reconnected. This tour will be completely dry, meaning *no* drugs or alcohol of any kind. This means *nothing* on stage, backstage, or on the RatHound busses."

"That won't be a problem," Chas assured.

The other band members heads involuntarily snapped toward Chas. We were by no means the biggest "party band" in history, but we were no angels either. We were young, knew how to have a good time, and were not unfamiliar with heavy drinking and colorful women. Since the overdose death of our original guitarist, we had done a pretty good job of keeping drugs away from us, but a *dry* tour? I, myself, wasn't convinced that every member of the band could or would be able to stick to those kinds of strict rules.

"After last night, I can't be sure that your band won't be a problem. My main role as RatHound's new manager is to protect their well-being and guard their sobriety. I also need to make sure that whoever goes on the road with us won't embarrass the band or bring on any bad press."

I was starting to understand the position Lucy was in and why she had been putting on her best "business face." Her father trusted her make decisions on behalf of a band that had been together for more than thirty years. He trusted her with their sobriety, and she did not want to let him down. She was clearly taking this new position very seriously, and for good reason. I had to get to know this woman. With every word she spoke, every moment that passed, I wanted more. More of *her*.

I took my glasses off in order to make eye contact with her, my hideous Rocky Balboa face be damned. "Miss Haddon," I said as genuinely as possible. "We won't let you down."

"Mr. Chambers," Lucy said to Chas, without taking her eyes off me. "I'd like to talk with Mr. Nelson alone for a moment."

My jeans tightened uncomfortably behind my zipper. I prayed to God she wouldn't ask me to get up and take a walk with her because my hard-on would have been fully visible. She probably already thought I was a creep, no need to confirm it.

"Alright lads, let's take a walk and give these two ladies some privacy," Chas said.

I hated Chas even more at that moment, but I was thankful I didn't have to get up. I still managed to flash him a nice "fuck you, you fat sausage roll of a man" kind of smirk as he passed.

I moved over one seat, partly in order to readjust the pressure in my pants, but mostly to be closer to Lucy. I didn't know what I was doing. I knew there was no way I could touch this woman—no way I could even go *near* this woman, but I also knew there was no way I could stay away from her.

"I didn't realize you were bringing the entire band," Lucy reiterated.

"Neither did I."

A shadow of a smile crossed her lips and I relaxed a little.

"So you didn't plan this," she deduced.

"No." I sighed. "Want to meet me for lunch later? Alone."

"For what purpose?"

"To talk. Privately. We can hash things out without prying eyes…or ears."

I watched her war with her emotions, transfixed. Everything she was thinking played out in the expressions on her face. Beautiful.

"I—"

"Before you say no," I said.

"I wasn't going to say no."

"You weren't?"

She shook her head. "I'll meet you at Billy's at one. It's two blocks north of here."

"I'll be there."

"Great." She rose to her feet and sauntered out the door without a backward glance, leaving me sitting there, once again watching her delicious ass walk away.

Zeke stalked back to the table. "What the hell? Why did she leave?"

"She had a meeting," I lied. "Don't worry, we'll see her tonight."

"If you fuck this up—"

"I'm not gonna fuck anything up," I hissed, and rose to my feet. "I'll see you tonight."

I walked out the door, uninterested in whatever else had crawled up my lead singer's ass.

Bam

BILLY'S DINER WAS buzzing with activity. The usually pleasant sounds of clanking plates and cups, and muffled conversations were an assault on my flaming skull. I wished we were in a quieter place, not just because of my headache, but because I wanted to block out everything except the voice of Lucy Haddon. How the fuck this woman had gotten into my head was beyond me.

"Mr. Nelson." Lucy's voice was low and serious, but I could hear tender nature under the surface. I swear I could taste the sweetness of her words as she spoke.

"Please call me Bam," I rasped, looking directly into her chocolate brown eyes.

"Mr. Nelson, I'm not sure you and I should get that close—"

"That close? I'm asking you to call me by my name, not marry me," I blurted out. Why did I say marry me? What the hell was wrong with me?

"What I mean"—she continued— "is that I'm not sure you and I will have many conversations after today. I wanted to speak with you alone because of the concerns I have about Roses for Anna." She pinned me with a stare. "My biggest one is you."

The way she looked at me made me feel like a little kid being scolded by a teacher. Despite this fact, I was irritatingly turned on. Then again, my eighth grade English teacher, Miss Abernathy yelled at me a lot and she was the subject of many school boy fantasies. I always thought it cruel that a bunch of horny teenage boys were asked to concentrate on the "Collected Works of Lord Percy Long Member" with Miss Abernathy's killer tits fighting to free themselves from her tight sweaters.

"You're a very talented musician, Mr. Nelson, and I respect the work you do, but it seems like your personal life might be interfering with your business life, which is no business of mine, of course, but I have to think about what's best for RatHound. We can't have your drama spilling into this tour. My father has trusted me to—"

"Miss Haddon…Lucy," I interrupted, speaking as softly and as gently as I could. I could tell she was disappointed in having to deliver this news and I couldn't stand to see her in pain any longer. "It's okay, I understand. You don't want to fail. You don't want to let your father or his band down, and when you look at me, you see a tabloid headline waiting to happen. It's a risk you can't take. *I'm* a risk you can't take. I get it. Thank you so much for your time."

With that, I stood up, took her hand in mine and shook it softly, then turned to walk out. I had no idea what my next move was going to be. It was supposed to be me convincing Lucy to include the band on the tour and here I was walking out on her.

What the hell was I going to tell the band? All I knew for sure was I had no excuses for the crazy events of my recent life and didn't want to hurt Lucy.

"Mr. Nelson, wait," Lucy called out somewhat restrained, still seated. I continued to move toward the door, keeping her in my peripheral and smiled when she stood and shouted, "Bam!"

My heart stopped along with my footsteps. I spun around slowly on the heels of my boots, trying to keep my mouth from grinning in triumph. Hearing Lucy say my name, and now seeing her standing across the room, made me want to close the gap between us more than I had ever wanted anything in my life. At that moment, I didn't care about the band, the tour, RatHound, Chas or anything else for that matter. I wanted to be with Lucy Haddon, and I wanted to hear her say my name every day.

"Yes, Lucy?" I challenged as I slowly walked

toward her, trying not to appear too eager.

She waved her hand toward the seat across from her. "Please sit down."

I did as instructed and she seemed to "reset" the conversation.

* * *

Lucy

I licked my lips and took a deep breath. Even with the nasty swelling and bruising on his face, Bam was one of the best looking men I'd ever seen.

"Mr. Nel—"

"Bam," he interrupted.

"*Bam*," I corrected. He shifted, leaning toward me and I studied him. He seemed so unbelievably sincere, but last night, he'd been a maniac.

"Lucy," he said, his voice sending shockwaves to my nether regions.

I cleared my throat and collected my thoughts. "My father seems to think you're the band for this tour."

"He's right."

"Why is he right?" I challenged.

"Because our music is a perfect fit for RatHound's, we bring an energy and talent that rivals theirs—"

"Conceited much?" I ground out.

"I'm stating facts, Lucy. I feel I can be honest with you." He smiled...slowly. I swallowed...convulsively. "I feel as though you're a straight shooter and I'm trying to be one as well."

"Fair enough." I mean, what else could I say? He wasn't wrong. Roses for Anna was one of the best bands in the world. Even if you didn't like their music (which would mean you were obviously an idiot, because they were amazing), no one ever disputed the level of talent.

"What you saw last night," Bam continued, "wasn't the norm. I don't make a habit of brawling with my manager, regardless of how much I dislike him."

This was interesting. From what I understood, Bam was very much at the helm of Roses for Anna, so I was surprised Chas was still around if he didn't like him.

"I will personally guarantee no drama," Bam finished.

"I'm not sure you have the power to guarantee that," I countered.

"Fair enough," he mimicked.

I smiled. I couldn't help it. He was charming. "I'll talk to Dad."

"Yeah?"

I nodded. "Yeah," I mimicked.

"Oh is *that* what I sound like?" He chuckled. "You're funny, Lucy."

"Thanks, Bam." Why his compliment sent a wave of warmth through my body, I had no idea, but I needed to get a handle on his affect on me.

"Give me your phone," he said.

"I'm sorry?"

He held his hand out. "Your phone. If you give it to me for thirty seconds, I'll give you something in return. Sound fair?"

I slid it toward him and he texted something then

handed it back. "You now have my personal cell. Text me when you talk to your dad."

"Your number, is that all I get?" I teased.

"Actually, I have something else for you," he said pulling a white envelope from his inside jacket pocket. "I would really like you to see us play tonight. Here's a ticket and full-access pass. I'm sure you'd have no problem getting in, but I'd really love for you to watch us from the side of the stage."

"Why is that? So you can show off for me?"

"No," Bam said, in his best drop-dead-sexy tone. "So I can see you better."

I shifted in my seat, willing my panties to stay on.

He continued, "We're also having a very small family shindig after the show, just the band, our road crew, and our families. It's very casual and nothing like last night. I'd love for you to join me."

And I'd like you to take me to the nearest broom closet and do unspeakable things to my body, but perhaps neither is a great idea at this time.

"I'll do my best to be at the show, and I'll certainly keep you in the loop on our decision." I tried hard to sound professional and emotionally unattached. I wondered if he could tell I wanted to crawl over the table and onto his lap.

He grinned. "Okay, Good."

I pushed away from the table and rose to my feet. He did the same. "Thank you for your time, Mister...I mean, Bam."

Bam leaned forward and kissed my cheek. "I'll talk to you soon."

I swallowed again and nodded, taking a slow,

deep breath. Without another word, I left the diner and slid into the Town Car.

"Home, Miss Haddon?" Sully asked.

"No. Can you take me to Mom and Dad's, please?"

"You bet."

While Sully drove to my childhood home, I stared at Bam's number now in my phone and thought about his kiss. I could still feel the scruff of his stubble as his lips touched my cheek. Gah! I needed to get a handle on this. I didn't typically react to men like this. I'd only had a couple of boyfriends and only one serious relationship in my life. That was in college and we'd broken up two years ago. We were still friendly, but Brad had never affected me the way Bam did.

I must be stressed and probably needed more sleep. I'd deal with the tour stuff and then maybe head to the beach for a couple of days. I'd been working nonstop for months…I needed a break. We pulled up to my parents' home and I headed inside.

My childhood home in Medina could only be described as opulent…Bill Gates was a neighbor, after all. The ten-bedroom, twelve-bath home was over thirteen-thousand square feet and was on five acres overlooking the water. My father had his own recording studio built on the property and the home and area didn't hide the fact we had money. The difference was, if you knew my parents, they were the most down to earth people on the planet and we were raised to respect everyone.

"Mom?" I called.

I heard her giggle and then my father's deep laugh and I walked toward the sound. As I approached the family room, more giggles escaped and I paused. "You better not be naked!" I warned.

"It's our house, baby girl," Dad called back. "If I want your mom naked, she'll be naked."

I wrinkled my nose knowing this statement was unfortunately true.

"Rex!" she admonished. "Come in, Luce. We're decent."

I walked into the family room and found them sitting very close on the sofa. Mom rose to her feet and pulled me in for a hug. "How's my girl?"

"I'm good, Mom." I hugged her back. "Same as I was yesterday."

Roxie MacDonald Haddon was big, blonde, and gloriously beautiful. She was bold in her personality and style, and she was adored by anyone who knew her…really knew her…which was hard to do. She was friendly, but she didn't let a whole lot of people "in."

She pulled away and cupped my face. "I don't like that you moved away."

"Ohmigod, Mom, I'm ten minutes from here."

"I'd rather you be within shouting distance."

Dad wrapped his arms around her waist from behind and grabbed her boobs.

"Rex!" she ground out at the same time I said, "Dad, gross, really?"

He laughed and kissed my mom's neck, then hugged me. "How did the meeting go?"

I flopped onto the sofa and filled them in… leaving out the kiss and my attraction to Bam.

"Works for me," Dad said.

"There's stuff going on there, though," I countered. "Chas is off."

"Chas is a dick," Dad agreed. "But as long as he doesn't screw up the tour, I don't really care."

I nodded. "Well, Bam has assured me they'll be on their best behavior, so…"

"Good job, Luce," Dad said. "I've got the contracts all ready to go."

"Of course you do," I breathed out. "And you want me to deliver them..."

"Tonight. At their show."

"Of course you do," I repeated.

"Is that okay?" Mom asked. "Or do you have plans?"

"I do have plans," I confirmed. "To take contracts to Roses for Anna to sign."

Dad grinned. "That's my girl."

"I'm going to the beach this weekend, though."

"You've earned it," Mom said.

"Coddling, Roxie," Dad admonished.

I chuckled. "You were the one who suggested it."

"Oh, right," he said.

"I need to head home and sort out something to wear."

"I'll grab the paperwork," Dad offered, and left the room.

"So," Mom began.

"So?"

"Bam Bam Nelson."

I rolled my eyes. "Ohmigod, Mom. He's…I don't

know…"

"Delicious?"

"So delicious."

She smiled. "He really is."

"You're not supposed to notice."

"Sweetness, your dad is everything to me and the sexiest man alive, according to me *and* People Magazine, but I'm not dead, so noticing that Bam Bam Nelson is also rather delicious is perfectly acceptable."

I giggled. "Okay, Mom. You weirdo."

Dad returned and handed me the contracts and I headed home. Sully was going to pick me up an hour before the show so I had over four hours to figure out what to wear.

Bam

HE FINAL SONG of the night is always my favorite part of the show. At this point, we've either got the crowd in the palm of our hands, or we've lost blood trying. On the nights when we've done our job well, and the audience has elevated the energy in the room, I can lose all control, while somehow also remaining in *complete* control. It's hard to describe, but ultimately the job of a drummer is to control chaos. Drummers are part timekeeper, part goalie, and part lion tamer. It's the drummer's job to make sure things on stage get out of hand, but not *too* out of hand.

"Okay, boys! Final song of the show—final show of the fucking tour. Let's do this!" I shouted to the band who were huddled around my drum riser in a sweaty mass. "Brother Electric!" I called out, making sure I'd made eye contact each band member before counting off the song.

"One, two, three, four," I howled while steadily bashing away on my hi-hat. We slammed into the song with full intensity. The song which I had written about Jimmy was one of our oldest, and I loved closing with it. Jimmy always had an intense energy about him that lit up a room. His internal amplifier was always set somewhere around nine, but he was looking for any opportunity to crank it to eleven. Jimmy had always been an important source of strength for me to draw from.

The band was in lockstep, just as we'd been all night. Maybe it was because it was the final night of the tour, or perhaps it had something to do with all the recent tension and fighting within the band. Oftentimes, the anger and passive aggressive shit that builds up in a band eventually explodes on stage, kind of like make-up sex after a heated fight. On the other hand, sometimes that tension shows itself in the form of an on-stage fist fight like it did in Toledo, Ohio. I hoped tonight would be better, especially knowing Lucy was somewhere backstage watching, so we'd better be on our best behavior.

> *"Electric brother, light my way,*
> *Mother mother, gone away."*

Zeke's voice rang out over the chaos on stage. The crowd sang along in full voice with their hands held high in the air. It's a truly flattering and humbling thing to have words that you wrote as a young man, in a time of extreme pain, being sung back to you by a crowd with such joy and exuberance.

I looked to my left and saw "Brother Electric" himself standing in his usual spot, at my ten o' clock, his bass slung low. I had never seen Jimmy have a bad show. Hell, I'd barely ever seen Jimmy have a bad day. He was a solid as they come, as bassist and as a friend.

"Shine your light on me!"

Edward, our guitarist and newest member was to my right, toward the front of the stage. As well as being a great guitar player, he was also an amazing painter. He was much quieter than the rest of the band, but was very easy to get along with and fit in well musically. I couldn't help but wonder how long he'd stick around. If our track record was any kind of indication—not long. Still, I really loved playing with him, and also appreciated that he could assist me with backing vocals.

"Brother Electric, shine your light on me!"

Zeke held out the final notes of the song. His tall, thin frame was stretched far out into the crowd, the toes of his boots barely touching the stage. He would give the crowd every bit of himself if he could. He would let them tear him to bits if it meant a better show. Zeke, for all his faults, is one of the most passionate and hardworking people I've ever known.

All night long, I had been very aware of an extra cup of gasoline being thrown on my fire. Her name was Lucy Haddon. Every time I thought about her watching tonight's show, it made me play harder and with more passion. I didn't want to impress her as much as I wanted to show her that Roses for Anna was the best possible band to open the upcoming reunion tour. There was something else though. I wanted her to see me play. I wanted her see a side of myself that is so important to who I am. I wanted her to see *me*.

The only problem was she was nowhere to be found.

She stood me up.

* * *

Lucy

I was frozen. Could. Not. Move. Ohmigod, this band was amazing. I had VIP privileges at most of the Seattle venues, and many others around the country and world, so I was currently second row center, alone, and transfixed.

Bam was one of the best drummers I'd ever seen or heard. He rivaled Jack Henry (RatHound's drummer) and I now knew why my dad wanted Roses for Anna to open the tour. Don't get me wrong, I'd always been a fan, but had never seen them play live. I was simply never in the same place the band was when they were performing. Had I known how good they were, I would have made more of an effort.

I had planned to make my way backstage partway

through their last song, but I couldn't make my feet cooperate with my heart. I wanted them to keep playing... *needed* them to keep playing. I could seriously watch Bam all night long...*God,* he was sexy as hell... and his background vocals were to die for. I don't think I'd ever understand the ability to sing and play drums at the same time. I'd been singing my whole life, and dad would pull me up on stage as a kid, but if I ever tried to add clapping or any other kind of percussive action, I lost the time. It was a running joke within RatHound.

The crowd went manic as the last note rang out and now I was stuck. No one knew who I was (I wore jeans, motorcycle boots and a dark blue hoodie so I was pretty nondescript in my appearance), which meant I couldn't motion to security and have them help part the mob for me to get through.

Crap!

* * *

Bam

She wasn't here. She didn't fucking show up. I wasn't sure what this meant about the tour, but I didn't even care about that right now. I wanted to see Lucy.

"What the fuck did you do?" Chas ground out, storming toward me.

"Excuse me?" I seethed.

"Lucy Haddon said she'd be here. So why isn't she, arsehole?"

"How the fuck should I know?" I toweled off and glared at him. "You were there. She was fine when she left the cafe."

Chas still didn't know about my clandestine meeting with Lucy at lunchtime, and he never would. But this confused me even more. I'd given her the backstage pass, we'd had a great conversation and connected on a friendly level, so why wasn't she here? I'd broken down her walls…or at least one.

I put distance between me and Chas, lest there be a repeat of the other night, and headed into the band room.

"So?" Zeke asked.

I shook my head. "She's not here."

"What the fuck did you do?"

"Back off, Zeke," Jimmy warned in his usual brotherly tone.

I sighed. "I didn't do anything. Maybe RatHound changed their mind."

Zeke scowled. "Or you pissed Lucy off and she changed it for them."

Maybe he was right. I flopped onto the sofa and dropped my head in my hands. It didn't matter how hard I tried to keep my life together, I managed to fuck it up when it counted the most. Just once, I'd like shit to work out.

"Sorry I'm late!"

My head whipped up at the sound of Lucy's voice and I shot off the couch. "Hey."

"Hi." She removed her hood and her red hair fell in sheets around her shoulders. "I got stuck in the crowd."

I gave Lucy a short hug. "What about the pass?" I

asked quietly, hoping the band wouldn't hear me.

She waved her hand dismissively. "I appreciated that, I did, but I wanted to be in the mix, you know? Feel the energy of the fans."

I nodded. I knew exactly what she meant.

"Hey, love," Chas greeted, leaning down to kiss her cheek.

Seeing her grimace, I once again closed the distance between us. I didn't want that asshole anywhere near her, particularly if she didn't want him near her.

"Thanks, Bam," she whispered, and I bit back a smile.

Those words were for my ears only and I relished them.

"So what did you think?" I asked, facing her.

Her cheeks pinked and I could tell she was trying not to give anything away. She was failing, but I let her have her secret...for the moment.

"It was really good," she said.

As I met her eyes, the world disappeared and it was just her and me standing in the green room. "Yeah?"

She nodded and rummaged in her bag. "I have the contracts."

"Contracts? So then..."

"Yes, Mister Nelson, RatHound would like to extend an official offer to join them as the support act on the summer tour."

Her smile lit me up more than the news. To play one show with RatHound was my fantasy as a sixteen-year-old kid, and now all I could think about was her. "Let me get the rest of the guys and you can tell 'em."

I returned quickly with the other three members and Chas, and Lucy relayed the good news. I assumed that's what she was doing because I heard nothing. Time seemed to slow, I couldn't look away from her, and for a moment I swear to God I forgot how to breathe.

"I'll take those," Chas said, breaking my focus as he greedily reached for the contracts.

I saw a flash of irritation cross Lucy's face, as she handed the paperwork to my manager. I took her arm gently and led her into the privacy of the hallway. "You okay?"

"I'm fine, why?" she asked, surprise in her voice.

"No reason. Just checkin' in. You look beautiful."

She blushed again. "Thanks. Um, I'm gonna head out. Chas can contact me if he has any questions."

"Hey, why're you runnin' away, Lucy?"

"Excuse me?"

I gave her a slow grin and she glanced at her feet. "You wanna get out of here?"

She squared her shoulders and raised an eyebrow. "And go where?"

"Somewhere quiet we can talk."

"I should really head home."

"Early day tomorrow?" I challenged.

"I'm heading to the beach actually."

"Sounds nice."

"It is."

Lucy bit her lip and I couldn't stop myself from

running my thumb over it and tugging it from her teeth. "Let's go get some pie."

Her eyebrows formed a V. "Pie?"

"You don't like pie?"

"I think my butt is proof positive I like pie," she retorted.

"Hey, I like your butt."

And I'd rather like to explore your pie.

That part I kept to myself, but I had a feeling she read my mind, because she blushed.

She licked her lips. "We're getting off topic."

"I know," I whispered. "I like it."

"Stop it," she rasped.

I chuckled. "Let me change real quick and we'll go get pie."

"Don't you have a meet and greet?"

"We did all that before the show, and I made sure we had no other business tonight."

"Five minutes, Luce," I said.

I didn't give her the chance to agree or disagree as I rushed back into the greenroom and grabbed a clean T-shirt.

* * *

Lucy

Bam walked away and I dragged my hands down my face. What the hell am I doing? It was past eleven…I shouldn't eat pie at this time of night. Yes, this was my first thought…not, I shouldn't have pie with Bam Bam Nelson, the man who made my panties melt away with his voice. No. It was that it was too late to eat pie. Ohmigod, I was a whore.

"Lucy?"

I looked up at Chas who slithered toward me. "Hey, Chas."

"I've looked over the contract, love, and everything looks great. I have one minor addition, but we can talk about that a little later in private."

"It's okay, I'm sure we're okay to speak here, what addition?"

"We need to add the lead singer bonus," he said a little quieter while gently guiding me to the back of the room. "Just standard stuff."

"Lead singer bonus?"

"Zeke, as many of today's front-men do, requires an additional five-thousand dollars per show—"

"Excuse me."

"I know you're new to management, love, but this is all standard boilerplate stuff these days," Chas said. "As the group's main focal point and draw factor, Zeke is entitled to a nightly performing bonus of five thousand dollars. This is built in to all of Roses for Anna's contracts."

I stared at him dumbfounded. "We don't do that Mr. Chambers."

"Well then, Roses for Anna *walks*."

Something was definitely hinky. Lead singer bonuses were *not* standard. I knew they happened, but they sure as hell weren't standard. This guy was as sleazy as they come, but I knew I had to play dumb a little. "Well, I certainly don't want that."

He smiled…like a snake. "No, love. Neither does your father."

"No," I agreed, and held my hand out. "Let me

take this back to our legal team and I'll get this corrected for you."

Chas handed me the contracts. "Excellent. Thanks, love."

I forced a smile and shoved the paperwork in my bag right as Bam walked back in. "Everything okay?"

"Yes. Great," I said.

"Are you staying for the party?" Chas asked.

"Lucy needs to get going," Bam answered for me.

"Yes, I do," I confirmed.

"I'm gonna walk her out," Bam said.

Chas looked a little nervous, but he seemed to shake it off and nodded. "See you in a bit, mate."

"Yep."

We headed to the back doors of the theater and Bam followed me out. I turned to face him and smiled. "Well, I'll see you—"

"I thought we were having pie."

I nodded toward the theater. "Didn't you just tell Chas you were going to the party?"

He shrugged. "I lied."

"Rebel," I retorted.

"You have *no* idea."

I grinned. "Sully is pulling around to pick me up…I guess you can tag along."

"Who's Sully?"

"My driver and bodyguard."

Bam stepped closer to me and took on a protective stance. "Shit, baby, you need a bodyguard?"

"No, not really. Not anymore, anyway," I admitted. "He's been with me since I was a kid and Dad likes him being around, so he's kind of stuck. It helps with the job." My phone buzzed and I saw Dad calling. "I have to take this."

Bam nodded and stepped away to give me a little privacy.

"Hey Dad."

"Hey, baby girl. Did you get the contract signed?"

"Chas wants a lead singer bonus."

"What the fuck?"

This came from Bam and I glanced up at him. "Um, Dad, can I call you right back?"

"Yeah, Luce, but we're not payin' a bonus," Dad said.

"I know. I'll call you right back." I hung up and faced Bam. "You didn't know about the signing bonus," I deduced.

He dragged his hands down his face and shook his head. "How much?"

"Five-thousand."

"I'm gonna fuckin' kill him." He headed back to the theater doors and pounded on the metal.

I texted Sully and let him know I'd be a while, then followed Bam inside.

Damn. I really wanted pie.

Bam

I DIDN'T KNOW exactly how I was going to murder Chas, but my plan was to make it slow and painful. How was I was going to deal with Zeke? How much did he have to do with this? I couldn't think about him now. I turned my focus back to Chas. I could only deal with one asshole at a time right now.

"Bam!" Hadley called, breathless as she jogged toward me.

"Not right now, Had."

"Wait, I really need to talk to you." She waved a

small stack of paperwork at me.

"What?" I snapped.

"I think Chas is stealing from the band."

I paused and took the paperwork from her, giving it a cursory glance.

"I'm Lucy," Lucy said, slightly out of breath.

I frowned. I didn't realize she'd followed me.

"Hi. I'm Hadley."

"Everything okay?" Lucy asked, placing her hand on my arm. Her voice was deep with concern. It calmed me long enough to remember my drama free promise to Lucy.

"I'm good, I just have to discuss this contract matter with Chas, right away." I wasn't about to storm into another after party in order to confront our manager in a fit of rage. At least I wasn't going to do that in front of Lucy. "Maybe we should grab that slice of pie another time. Thank you again for coming and for everything. I'm sure we'll get this whole contract thing sorted out. We'll talk soon." I left the two women standing there, and continued my quick, but controlled walk down the hall.

* * *

Lucy

I smiled at Hadley. "You found something hinky, huh?"

She nodded. "I can't talk about it, but yeah, I did."

"Totally get it. I'm going to make a quick call, will you excuse me?" I grabbed my phone and called my dad back.

"Hey, Luce."

"Hey Dad." I filled him in on everything I knew and he swore.

"That poor bastard."

"Which one?" I asked.

"For the moment, Bam. But Chas is gonna be ruined."

"He deserves it."

"Don't disagree."

I sighed. "So, what do you want me to do?"

"Get Bam to sign. We'll need to get his legal name, but let's give him a few days to deal with all this shit."

I nodded. "Okay. I'll take care of it."

"Good job, honey."

"Thanks Dad."

I hung up and noticed Hadley was no longer in the hallway. I was alone and unsure exactly what to do. Since I didn't feel any of this was my business, I figured heading home was the best course of action, so I walked outside and slid into the Town Car.

"Home, Miss Haddon?" Sully asked.

"Yes, please, Sully. Thanks."

As Sully drove me home, I texted Bam and let him know we'd talk when things calmed down.

"Sully? Can we stop at PCC real quick please?"

"Sure thing."

I still had a hankering for pie…and maybe some ice cream.

* * *

Bam

"You piece of shit!" The words flew out of my

mouth as I approached our manager.

"Not this bullshit again," Zeke angrily whined as he slammed his champagne glass down.

"Shut the fuck up, Zeke! I'll deal with you next!"

"Deal with me? You'd better back the fuck off, man!

"Both of you chill the hell out!" Jimmy ordered, immediately placing himself between us. This certainly wasn't the first time the three of us had found ourselves in this situation.

However, regardless of all the fights we'd had over the years, I'd never felt betrayed by Zeke before. The hurt I felt was even worse than the anger. I understood Chas ripping us off, but how could Zeke get him to do this, and why?

"A lead singer bonus?" I seethed.

Zeke's posture softened and his eyes dropped as he backed up a few steps.

"Look, man, it's not a big deal," Zeke said dismissively.

"Not a big deal to you! Why would it be with five thousand extra dollars in your pocket after every show?"

Jimmy and Edward had now turned their full attention to Zeke. Chas remained totally silent, which was my first indication that things were worse than I thought.

"Five thousand dollars a night—what is he talking about Zeke?" Jimmy's words were controlled but intense. Jimmy was the nicest guy in the world—until he wasn't.

"I don't know what the fuck you're talking about,

Bam. I don't know anything about five thousand dollars. Chas said he was going to negotiate a lead singer bonus for me. He said it was something that all his bands did, and that I'd get an extra two grand for the whole tour. I figured if this is what the other singers were doing, why not me? You get an extra slice from songwriting, and Jimmy has his studio, so why not get mine?"

I turned to Chas who was now visibly uncomfortable. I had never seen Chas squirm before, not in the slightest, but his fat face was beet red and his forehead was covered in sweat.

"You're gonna tell me exactly what the hell is going on right now," I said flatly. I was glad I had sent Lucy home.

Chas began to stammer out his first words. "Look lads, there's clearly been a mistake here. I'll talk to Lucy—"

"You'll stay the fuck away from Lucy Haddon or I'll break every bone in the sausage casing you call a body." I could see the band's attention turn toward me. My protectiveness for Lucy was obviously on display.

Keep your cool.

"I'll ask you one more time," I warned. "What the hell is this lead singer bonus shit, and what have you told Zeke?"

"I'll tell you what he's been doing and what he was planning." Hadley came through the door, the stack of papers held high above her head.

"That little tart doesn't know anything!" Chas bellowed toward Hadley.

I jabbed a finger toward him. "Shut your mouth or I'll let Winston lock you in a road case."

"Just say the word, brother," Winston rasped from about four feet behind me.

Hadley continued, "He's been skimming a thousand dollars a night from the band in the form of hidden management fees as well. He probably knew he wouldn't be able to hide this much longer, so devised a new scam for this tour. He knew about the RatHound tour possibility a month ago but never said anything about it because he needed time to work on Zeke."

"I swear, Bam, he told me it was a one-time payment of two thousand bucks! I was pissed at you and shouldn't have done it, but I had nothing to do with this other shit!" Zeke said.

I believed him, and although I was still angry, I could see he had been played by Chas.

"You stole from me, Chas. You stole from my brothers. You lied to us, tried to turn us against each other, and thought you'd get away with it?" I asked.

"You ungrateful little shits would be nowhere without me. You have no idea how the real world works. I take what I earn. What I deserve!" Chas bellowed, spit flying from his mouth.

"Chas, you're fired."

The words had barely left my mouth when Winston and two members of our road crew grabbed Chas in order to "assist him" out of the room.

"Hold on!" I called out as they reached the doorway. "Winston, call Mack and see if the Dogs of Fire have some Seattle members that could babysit that piece of shit for a little while. Ask him to dig up anything else he can on Chas while he's at it. The man is part bloodhound and I want to know everything I can about Chas before calling the lawyers. I also want to get back every cent that piece of shit stole from us. Tell Mack I'll owe him—again."

"You heard the man," Winston rasped to the roadies. "Now, let's go see how well you fit in that road case." Chas barely had time to begin his groveling before he was removed from the room.

The band was silent, but Jimmy and Zeke looked at me knowingly. I'd met Mack when I did the duet with Melody. She was starring in a near X-rated movie based off of Mack's wife's novel and Mack and I had stayed in touch. Involving the Dogs was not something I really wanted to do, but we had history with them, and they knew how to show restraint and discretion. As motorcycle clubs went, the Dogs of Fire tended to be above board and had always been supportive of us. A couple of the younger recruits had even acted as roadies and security for a couple of shows in Portland, all put together for us by Mack.

Hadley approached me quietly. "Bam?"

"Yeah, Had?"

"Um, so I kind of did something."

I rubbed my forehead. "I don't know that I can handle much more, Hadley."

She smiled. "I siphoned some of the money Chas stole into a secret account."

"Excuse me?"

"I wanted to get it away from him before I brought

this to you, so I kind of did it without him knowing." She grimaced. "I was able to get almost sixty-percent back so far…I know it's not the best out—"

I dragged her against me and gave her a bear hug. "Are you shittin' me?"

"I learned how to forge his signature," she whispered. "I hope this doesn't get me in trouble."

I met her eyes. "Babe, if anyone comes lookin' for you, you'll have the full support of the band and our legal team. This won't touch you. As a matter fact, you're the only one I can trust right now. Just do me a favor and stick around and we'll get all this sorted out."

She grinned. "Okay, Bam. Thanks. I'm going to head back to the party, okay?"

"Absolutely."

I grabbed a bottle of Maker's Mark from the bar, and declared "band meeting" before exiting.

* * *

Lucy

I took one last bite of the chocolate cream pie I'd purchased and rinsed my plate. It was exactly what I wanted, but it didn't quite "satisfy" since I'd really wanted to eat it while staring at Bam. I glanced sadly at the rest as I slid the box into the fridge.

Just some extra empty calories to add to all the rest of late.

Damn, I loved me some pie. Of course, if I were being self-aware, I might recognize I was eating my feelings, but tonight I chose to be oblivious.

As I poured a glass of wine and started my wind-down time, my phone buzzed. I let out a rather pathetic whimper. I'd left my phone on my kitchen island and I really didn't want to get back up…it was wine time. *But*…I was technically awake and the call might be important, so I hauled my ass up and answered the phone without looking at the caller ID. "This is Lucy Haddon."

"Hey, it's Bam."

"Hi." My heart raced a little. His voice was even sexier over the phone. "Is everything okay?"

He sighed. "Yeah. Just wanted to hear your voice."

I bit my lip. I should object. I should tell him to call someone who wasn't in a business relationship with him. One of his friends, perhaps. I should keep this professional.

Instead, I asked, "That bad?"

"Little bit."

"Sorry, Bam."

"It's too late to meet me for pie, huh?"

"Little bit," I mimicked.

I heard the smile in his voice when he asked, "What about meeting me for breakfast tomorrow around ten?"

"Most people eat breakfast well before ten, Bam," I pointed out.

"Brunch, then?"

I grinned. "I guess I could bring you new contracts before I head to the beach."

"Yeah, about that. We're gonna have to remove Chas from any contracts, as his services are no longer required by Roses for Anna."

"Sounds like we have a few things to talk about."

"Indeed we do. I'm in communication with our lawyer and the label and for now I'll be taking point on all business matters."

"I can have new contracts drawn up, but I'll need your legal name so you can sign them."

"Beau Nelson."

Ohmigod, the man's name was Beau? Sexy name for a sexy southerner. Crap on a stick!

"But nobody ever calls me that," he added. I was relieved to be rid of Chas, but so nervous to know that I'd be dealing with Bam even more directly and frequently.

"Okay, I'll get those sorted," I said as professionally as I could. "Which means, the only question now is where to meet for brunch tomorrow."

"I'll take you wherever you'd like to go, baby," Bam replied.

"You can't call me 'baby,' Bam."

"No?"

"No," I breathed out. Damn it! I needed to be firm, but I my voice was all quivery and crap.

"How come?"

"Because we have a professional relationship."

"So, I can't call you 'baby' because we have a professional relationship?"

"Exactly."

"You're fired, then."

I let out an inelegant snort. "You can't fire me. I don't work for you."

"Then we don't, *technically*, have a professional relationship."

"*Bam*." I dropped my head back with a groan.

"Meet me for *brunch,* I'll sign the contracts, then our professional relationship will be done and we can have some real fun."

"What kind of a girl do you think I am?" I challenged. "I don't fraternize with the opening act."

"Never?"

"Never," I confirmed.

"So fraternizing is out…what's your position on canoodling?"

"Frowned upon."

"Tom-foolery?" he challenged.

I bit back a laugh. "That's *right* out."

"Well, shit, you're not givin' me much to go on here…*baby.*" He sighed again…dramatically. "I guess you'll simply have to meet me for brunch and we'll stick to some light shenanigans."

Well, crap on a stick. The man was funny. I was a sucker for funny. Especially drop-dead gorgeous drummers who offered me pie.

"Light shenanigans I can handle," I said. "Where do you want me to meet you?"

"Billy's again? Say, eleven?"

"I can do that."

"Great. I'll see you tomorrow. Dream of me."

"Ohmigod, Bam, you're ridiculous."

He chuckled. "Yeah?"

"Yes, definitely."

"But I just put that in your head which means you'll be frustrated in the morning."

I gasped. "I will not."

"Yeah, Lucy, you will," he countered. "And I'll be happy to take care of that for you."

"This conversation falls under tom foolery, Bam."

"Okay." He laughed. "I'll see you tomorrow."

"Goodnight." I hung up, finished my wine, and headed to bed.

And I dreamed of Bam. Shit.

Lucy

BILLY'S DINER WAS surprisingly busy, but as I walked in, I saw Bam stand and give me a chin lift. I licked my lips and gave myself an internal talking to.

Must keep my panties on…must keep my panties on.

I headed to the table and Bam gave me a slow, sexy smile as I approached him. "Hey."

"Hi," I rasped, then cleared my throat. Good lord, I needed to get a grip.

"I ordered you a non-fat latte with one shot of caramel."

"Oh, wow, that was nice." He remembered. Ohmigod, I was in trouble. "Thanks."

He leaned down and kissed my cheek then we took our seats. I pulled the contracts out of my purse and handed them to him and took a sip of my coffee. Perfect.

"I'll take a look at these with the lawyer and get them right back to you. You hungry?"

"I'm always hungry," I admitted.

"What do you want?"

"Blueberry muffin, please."

He grinned and motioned for the waiter. "A blueberry muffin for the lady and a side of extra crispy bacon for me please."

While he procured our food, I checked over the contracts, texted my dad to let him know everything was in order, and then slid the paperwork back into my bag.

The waiter returned with the charred remains of what was perhaps once bacon, and the biggest muffin I'd ever seen. "I don't know that I'm *that* hungry."

He chuckled. "We'll share."

"Good plan. I'm not sure your bacon can even be considered edible." I grabbed the knife and cut the cakey goodness in half.

"What are you talking about?" he asked. "This bacon is absolutely perfect."

"If you say so." I chuckled. "What are your plans now that you have a couple of months off?" I asked handing him the muffin half.

"The guys in the band are takin' off tomorrow.

Headed back to Alabama."

"You said, 'the band.' Does that not include you?"

He shook his head. "I'm kind of liking Seattle. Thinkin' of sticking around."

I nearly choked on my coffee. "You're staying in Seattle?"

Bam leaned back in his chair like he didn't have a care in the world. "That all depends on you."

"Excuse me?"

"I'd like to get to know you on a personal level, Lucy."

"I don't think that's a good idea."

"Why not?"

I didn't really have an answer for him. At least not a legitimate one. I'd only had one serious boyfriend my entire life to date… ergo, I'd only slept with one man. As confident as I was, I was still somewhat sheltered and probably even a little naive. My dad and Sully had made sure of that. I wasn't a virgin by any means, but I guess you could say I was "virgin adjacent."

Getting to know Bam would more than likely wreck me. The man had a sex tape for crying out loud! I bit my lip. "I really think we need to keep this professional."

"You're scared."

I closed my eyes and took a deep breath. "Are you always like this?"

"Like what?"

I studied him. "A pain in the ass."

"Pretty much," he said with a cocky grin.

"Look, we have a six week tour coming up where we'll be in each other's space almost every day."

"So?"

"*So*, I think that'll give us plenty of time to get to know each other, don't you?" I challenged.

He leaned forward and shook his head. "I want to get to know you while things are quiet. When we're not distracted. When we can focus on who we are as people…not as people in the business."

"I'm not a musician."

"That's not what I hear. Word on the street is you've got a voice."

I felt the heat creep up my neck. "Stop it."

"Just telling you what I've heard. I look forward to hearing that voice for myself soon."

"Not…gonna…happen," I whispered.

"So," he continued. "Spend the rest of the weekend with me."

"I'm going to the family beach house," I reminded him. "Which I still haven't packed for."

"Sounds fun."

"Are you angling for an invite?"

He shrugged. "Angling for an invite to spend a few days with a beautiful woman at the beach? No, why would I do that?"

I sighed. "Bam, I don't know you."

He raised his hands as if to surrender. "We can stay in separate rooms. Hell, I'll sleep on the floor like a dog. No funny business, I promise."

"Because serial rapists never say that," I muttered under my breath, then realized what I'd said. "Not that I'm saying you're—"

He laughed. "Baby, I get it. No offense taken."

"Stop calling me baby."

"I'm not gonna do that, Lucy."

"Why the hell not?" I snapped.

"Because you like it."

I *did* like it. Damn it!

I took a deep breath. "I'm not going to the beach with you alone, Bam."

"Hold up. You were going to the beach *alone* without me?"

"Yes."

"Hell no."

"Excuse me?"

He frowned. "In what universe did your father think it was a good idea to let you go to the beach alone?"

"I'm not a child, Bam."

"I'm aware you're not a child. You're a fuckin' drop-dead gorgeous woman who shouldn't be driving out to a remote beach house alone," he ground out. "It's not safe."

"Ohmigod, are you for real?" I hissed. "You don't know me. You don't know my father and this conversation is over."

I rose to my feet, but he grabbed my arm. "My mom was murdered, Lucy."

I gasped. "What?"

"When I was seventeen." He tugged on my hand gently. "Sit down and I'll explain."

I lowered myself back into my chair, my heart breaking for him.

"It was my fault."

"You murdered her?"

"No. But she was out alone at night because of me."

I swallowed. "Bam—"

He shook his head. "Don't, Lucy. I don't want your pity."

I wasn't going to give him my pity, but I figured I should let him talk without interruption. "Sorry, Bam. I'm listening."

"No, I'm sorry," he said on a sigh. "It's just people treat you differently when they find out your mother has been murdered. I learned early on to sidestep questions about her and never bring up her murder to anyone."

"What was her name?"

"Anna."

My eyes widened. "So the band *was* named after her? I've heard so many different stories over the years about the origin of the band's name."

"I never wanted to talk about this stuff to the press, so I'd make up different stories whenever asked. The band understood and loved seeing me mess with reporters."

"So your mom's favorite flowers were roses, I assume?"

"I have no idea what her favorite flowers were. My father sure as fuck never bought her any. When she died, I remember wanting to have flowers to put on her casket, so I took all the money I had and bought her roses. I wanted the last thing that I could do for her be meaningful."

"That's really nice, Bam."

He shrugged. "It wasn't about being nice…it was all I could do for her. So when the band needed to choose a name, I wanted to call it Roses for Anna because I needed her to be remembered and I needed my music to be connected to her and the memory of her. My band had become by family and the road my home, but I knew that if she'd lived, she would have supported whatever I did."

"So how did she die?"

"Nobody really knows, the police sure as hell gave up looking for answers a long time ago. My piece of shit truck had broken down, yet again, and my dad had been on my ass about getting a job and getting it fixed. I kept telling him I didn't have time for a job because of the band and I just needed to wait it out for the next big show so I could make the repairs, but the truck broke down before that happened, leaving me stranded. And since Dad was drunk, Mom came to get me…only she never arrived."

I squeezed his hand, but didn't speak.

"They found her body about five miles away from where I'd broken down, in a field. She'd been shot and her car and belongings were never seen again."

I bit back tears. He didn't want my pity, but how else are you supposed to feel when someone loses their mother so young?

"We never found out who killed her or why."

"Wow," I whispered. "That must have been devastating."

"So, I'm sorry if I sound like an asshole, but I

don't like knowing you're driving somewhere alone, especially at night."

"Well, I was supposed to leave this morning, but someone made me meet him for brunch."

"Not funny, Lucy."

I sighed. "Not that it's any of your business, but Sully's going to drive me. He always does. And he stays in the guest house at the edge of the property. I'm never really alone. And it's barely an hour away"

He nodded. "Okay, good."

I reached over and squeezed his arm. "I'm really sorry about your mom, Bam."

His jaw flexed as he gave another quick nod.

I couldn't believe what I was about to say. "Separate rooms, Sully's on watch and knows how to kill a man in less than ten seconds, so if you try anything…"

"Lucy Haddon, are you inviting me to join you at your beach house?" he teased, seeming relieved we'd changed the subject. "I'm not sure I want to go. In fact, I think I have plans."

I smiled.

"Ohmigod, you just beat your chest like Tarzan demanding I take you, and now you're bailing on me?"

"Tarzan? Oh, and I suppose that makes you Jane?"

"No that makes me leaving," I retorted, and rose to my feet. "I'll be at your hotel in two hours. Be there and be packed."

I headed out the door and into the Town Car before he could reply. "Home to pack, Sully, then we're going to pick Bam up at his hotel."

"For what purpose, Miss Haddon?"

"He's coming to the beach house."

Sully turned to face me. "Excuse me?"

I jabbed a finger at him. "Don't start. I know you and Dad did a background check on all of them, so if Bam was a concern, I would have been warned to stay away. Neither of you have done that, so stow it."

He rolled his eyes and faced front again, turning on the car.

"And don't call Dad and tattle on me."

"I don't tattle, Miss Haddon."

"Don't tattle, my ass," I retorted. "Walker Wynns ring a bell?"

Walker was a guy I'd met at a show about four years ago. We'd dated for a few weeks and he'd wanted to take me to Portland for the weekend, but Sully had gone to my father and all hell had broken loose.

"His name was Walker, Miss Haddon."

"So?"

"*So*, he was no Texas Ranger, I can assure you of that."

I bit back a giggle. "Be that as it may, it's my life, and as an adult, I should be allowed to make my own mistakes."

"I will keep that in mind, Miss Haddon."

We arrived at my apartment and Sully parked the car.

"I'm serious, Sully. Do not call Dad."

"I won't, Miss Haddon. You have my word," he said, and walked me up to my apartment.

He kept his word, but the bastard called my mother.

* * *

"Ohmigod, Mom, Sully promised," I snapped and zipped up my bag.

"I believe he promised not to call your dad, honey."

"Well, he and I are going to have to have a conversation about semantics."

She chuckled. "Look, I just want you to be smart."

"I *am* smart, so if you have a genuine concern, please let me know now or forever hold your peace."

"I don't, Luce. I really don't. Dad and I don't want you to get hurt."

"I appreciate that, Mama, I really do. But we're going as friends and nothing's going to happen."

"He's gorgeous, baby girl."

"I'm aware."

"And you know I could never resist your father."

"I'm also aware, but you raised me right, Mom. Not to mention, Sully's always within shouting distance."

"Well, I can't argue with that."

I smiled. "Would you give Luke this much grief if he wanted to take a girl to the beach house for the weekend?"

My brother was two years older than me and almost as protective as my father.

"Your brother has a black belt in karate, honey. You have a black belt in over complicated coffee. Theoretically, he can kill a man with his bare hands…you, however, can't kill with one shot of caramel flavoring."

I burst out laughing. "You are ridiculous."

"Just keep your wits about you, Lucy."

"I will, Mom, I promise."

"I'll talk to you on Tuesday."

"Sounds good. Love you."

"Love you, too, honey."

Mom hung up and I headed out of my apartment. Sully was waiting in the hallway.

"You suck."

He took my bag with a smile. "I didn't call your father, Miss Haddon."

"In the future, no tattling to my father, my mother, or my brother."

He grinned wider. "We'll see."

I climbed into the car and we headed to Bam's hotel.

* * *

Bam

Lucy's driver/butler/terminator placed my duffle bag into the trunk of his Town Car and gave me a polite but somewhat icy smile.

"Thanks a lot. Sully right?" I asked while extending my hand.

"That's right, Mr. Nelson," he said while firmly closing the handshake. His intense gaze never leaving mine. "Let's get on the road, shall we, sir?"

"Bam."

"Excuse me sir?"

"You can call me Bam or Bam Bam. No need for sir or Mister. Bam's fine. You know "You can't spell Alabama without B.A.M.!"

Sully blinked slowly.

I immediately started sweating. "It was a thing a few years ago, a sort of slogan." Suddenly I felt like I was meeting her dad. "Y'know what, never mind."

"We don't want to hit traffic Mr. Nelson."

What the hell was up with these people and their formal address? I felt like I was in one of Miss Abernathy's Lord Percy Long Member plays. I gave up and got in car.

This is going to be a long ride.

Bam

FTER HITTING TRAFFIC and spending over an hour on the road, we arrived at the Haddon family beach house in Alki Point. I had seen many beach houses in my time. We had crashed and partied at surfer pads, crab shacks, and bungalows up and down the Gulf Coast, but I had never seen anything like this.

"This is your beach house?" I exclaimed as we pulled into the driveway.

"My family's beach house, yes."

"How many other families live here?" I asked with a chuckle.

"The Sullynator" parked the car and effortlessly hoisted our bags out of the trunk. It made me wonder how many bodies he'd pulled from that trunk in a similar fashion while on the job.

"It's only a six bedroom house, Bam." Lucy smiled as we stepped out of the car.

"Those must be some big ass rooms. You have your own lighthouse for cryin' out loud!"

"This is true." She giggled. "Mom keeps threatening to add on. She's preparing for grandkids. Whatever. I love it here. I've been coming here all my life and sometimes I just forget to stop and look around at everything around me."

She wasn't kidding. There was much to appreciate here. The house sat on a bluff overlooking Puget Sound, with a private staircase directly to the beach. It was beautiful, but I could barely take my eyes off Lucy. The car ride here had been torture. To sit so close to her but not be able to touch her was killing me. I had never wanted a woman more in my life.

"You know what your problem is?" I asked while walking her to the front door. "You're too serious."

"*I'm* too serious?" she asked while unlocking the front door. The front alarm sensor beeped and Lucy punched in the access code on the nearby panel. "Who are you to judge, what with your *rage issues* and all?"

I looked down at my knuckles and smirked. "No, seriously, you said it yourself. You don't ever stop working long enough, to appreciate what you have."

"Ummmm, I don't think that's exactly what I said."

"Close enough. Here's my point," I continued. "We're here now, and there's a beautiful beach just down there, so why not take the time to appreciate this night, and more importantly my charming company."

Lucy let out a soft laugh and bit her lip.

"Will that be all, Miss Haddon?" Sully asked briskly, instantly breaking the moment.

"Yes, Sully, thank you for everything. See you in the morning," she said. Sully gave me a slow nod and headed left. I watched him walk to the small home on the edge of the property, presumably to clean his gun.

"Let's get our coats and hats on. It's cold out there," Lucy suggested.

While Lucy rummaged in the closet for outerwear, I took in the house. From the outside it looked much like the other upscale sea-side properties in the area. The interior was another matter. The Haddon's had forgone the typical sea shells and anchors motif and designed the interior to look and feel like a log cabin style hunting lodge. With huge picture windows overlooking the water, it was magnificent.

Lucy handed me a leather jacket that probably belonged to her brother and we donned our coats then headed down to the water. The beach was nearly deserted. It was late in the afternoon and the winter air kept most beachgoers away. The violent grey waters crashed against the rocky shoreline as the sun began its descent. The two of us walked side by side, and Lucy resumed our conversation from the diner.

"What happened after your mom's death?" Lucy

asked.

"Dropped out of high school, hit the road with the band. The rest is history."

"What about your dad?"

"What about him?" I snapped. She looked hurt and I immediately felt like a dick. "Sorry. I didn't mean to snap. The memories are shit at times."

"We don't need to talk about this."

"I want to." She raised an eyebrow in challenge and I sighed. "I do, seriously. It's just no one knows this outside of the band, and it's not a story I've ever had to tell, if you know what I mean."

"Because the band was there while it was happening," she deduced.

I nodded. "The truth is my dad was an asshole. Always had been. Drunk most nights, shoved my mom more than once, hit her a couple times, but she wanted to keep us together, so she stayed. When she died, he kicked me out and I haven't seen or talked to him since."

"What do you mean he kicked you out?"

"My old man and I never saw eye-to-eye anyway, and when my mom died, he blamed me. I blamed myself so I couldn't really argue with him. He wanted me out and I wanted to be gone, so that was that."

"And you haven't spoken to him since? I can't imagine not speaking with my dad."

She looked genuinely heartbroken for me. Not just about my mother, but about my father as well. I had spent a lot of time grieving for my mother, but I guess I never thought much about the fact that I had lost what little I had of him as well. Shit, I didn't even know if the bastard was still alive.

"He pretty much ignored my mother, when he wasn't yelling at her in a drunken rage, so I could never figure out why he even cared when she died. I was just a kid who'd lost the only person who cared about me, and that prick wanted me on the street, so I split."

"I'm so sorry, Bam, I really am." Lucy's words were soft and yet cut deeply into me. Her empathy and honesty were almost too much to take.

"It's okay," I continued. "The band became my family and the road became my home. It's pretty much been that way ever since." I shifted gears. "What about you? What was your childhood like? It must have been pretty amazing, right? Growing up among rock royalty?"

"Amazing, yes…up to a certain point, then crazy, then really hard," she said. "I grew up on the road too. In all of my earliest memories, we were on the road with RatHound. Jack and Mitch are my uncles and Mitch's wife and kids are my aunt and cousins. Not to mention, the road crew guys who were always there to get us into, or keep us out of trouble."

"I can't ever imagine you being any trouble, baby."

"Bam, you really can't call me that." Lucy turned to face me.

I took her hands in mine. "I think I've been perfectly clear that I like you very much. I call you baby, because I love the way the micro-expressions in your face change when I do."

I felt Lucy's hands tremble and I held them tighter while pulling her closer to me. "I know you're scared, and I can think of half a dozen reasons why you should be. Hell, I'm scared too, but I know how I feel about you."

"Bam, you don't understand. I can't get involved with you—with any musician for that matter."

I knew one of the reasons she was so afraid. Her father and RatHound guitarist Mitch "Robbie" Roberts had both had very public battles with heroin.

"When I was eleven years old, my mom told me and my brother that dad was sick. She assured us that he was going to be okay, but would be away in a hospital for a few weeks. I didn't see my father for three months, and he didn't come home for good for another year."

"I understand Lucy, but I'm not your father. I'm not Rex Haddon."

"Maybe not, but you don't know how much you're like him. Sometimes I really like that about you, but sometimes it scares the crap out of me. The passion you have for your music, for your life, is a lot like my dad, and that passion almost burned him up. The road, the drugs, the anger, the isolation—it destroyed his band, nearly ended his marriage and almost cost him his life."

"Lucy, I promise I won't let this life, or anything in it, destroy you...or me," I avowed as I desperately pulled her closer. Our bodies were pressed tightly against each other as I leaned in to kiss her. Our lips met and I heard her moan softly. I cupped her face and deepened the kiss. Her skin was warm but I burned for her as I tipped her head back slightly.

* * *

Lucy

Holy crap on a stick, the man could kiss. Shit. I was worried about how his voice affected me…but now his tongue made me long for more.

I had to get a handle on this.

But in a minute.

Right now I wanted to explore his mouth. Truth be told, I wanted to explore more than his mouth, but for the moment, I'd settle for lips…and his tongue.

Ohmigod, his tongue. He was an expert with his tongue.

Why do I keep obsessing on his tongue?

I couldn't stop a giggle which forced me to break the kiss.

Bam raised an eyebrow. "My kisses make you laugh?"

I licked my lips and shook my head. "Sorry. They don't. They're nice."

"They're *nice*?" He dropped his hands. "Damn, baby, I was hoping for something a little better than *nice*."

I could feel the heat creep up my neck and I groaned. "If you really want to know, I couldn't stop thinking about your tongue and how amazing it was. I kept obsessing on it and then I realized how weird it was that I kept obsessing on it."

He grinned and slid his hand to my neck. "Obsessing, huh?"

"No. Nope. You need to let that go. Because this is *not* a good idea."

"Something you need to know about me…I don't let things go." He kissed my cheek, then the other. "Especially when I meet someone as special as you."

"Bam," I whispered.

"I'm gonna stick around a while, Lucy. We're gonna get to know each other and then at the end of the tour, we can decide where to go from there, sound good?"

"I don't know—"

"Nodding is a good way to go here, baby."

"I don't have time for a relationship, Bam."

"Then we'll take it slow. We have a couple days to get to know each other without interruption…and no sex. Kissing, however, is on the table…and maybe some light petting."

"Ohmigod, stop," I rasped.

He grinned. "You'd rather some heavy petting?"

"Bam," I breathed out, and dropped my head to his chest. "You need to stop talking. I can't resist you when you're talking."

"I can kiss you instead," he offered.

"No. Absolutely not." I met his eyes. "I need you to stop doing both."

"How do we get to know each other if I can't talk?"

"Charades."

Bam dropped his head back and laughed. "Shit, you're funny."

"I wasn't trying to be funny." I rubbed my arms

and smiled. "But I'm glad you think so."

"You cold?" he asked, and shrugged off his jacket, slipping it over my shoulders.

"Ohmigod, you're a gentleman as well?" I complained. "Just stop all of this."

Bam laughed again. "How about we head back to the house and light the fire?"

I nodded. "Sounds good. We'll do it silently, though."

He grinned and took my hand.

Oh, yeah, 'cause that makes things better.

I sighed. I was screwed.

Bam

AS WE APPROACHED the stairs leading back to the house, I made sure to fall a few steps behind Lucy. I didn't want to miss an opportunity to watch her luscious ass as she walked up the stairs. She looked back briefly and busted me admiring God's handy-work.

"Are you looking at my butt?" she asked, fighting back a smile.

"Looking at your butt? No, baby," I replied matter-of-factly. "I'm *staring* at your *ass*."

"What? That's the same thing!" she protested.

"No ma'am. Apparently you're unaware of the

ancient studies of Assery."

"Assery?" she asked flatly. "Really?"

"Yes, ma'am, a very serious pursuit that I have devoted the better part of my thirty years to, and I'd ask you kindly to show a little more respect to the ancient ways."

"The ancient ways of Assery?"

"More like a way of life… a spiritual path if you will."

"It sounds made up…and I know you're lying because you're not thirty. Your birthday isn't for another two months."

"Whoa, stalker much?"

"Don't change the subject," she retorted, as we reached the top of the stairs.

"Please stop interrupting until we conclude our very serious theological discussion."

"Theological, huh?"

"Well, ass-a-logical."

"Please continue," she said.

"While all women posses posteriors, most do not know that these posteriors all fall into one of four categories.

"Really, is this what you think?"

"It's irrelevant what I think," I instructed. "This wisdom has been passed down to southern men from the ages. This is law."

She opened the front door with an exaggerated bow and wave. "Please enter and proceed, oh wise one."

I walked through the door, took her hand, and kissed it. I wasn't sure how long the Sullynator needed to recharge his battery pack, but I hoped we wouldn't see him again tonight. "Now, as I was saying"—I continued—"according to the Laws of Assery the four categories of rear ends are as follows; butts, tushes, asses and rumps."

"*Rumps?*" Lucy burst out laughing.

"Yes, rumps, Miss Haddon, but that topic is perhaps a bit too advanced for you. We'll just focus on the first three for now. Butts are fine, but are sort of the 'stock factory model' of rear ends. A nice butt will do in a pinch, no pun intended…"

Lucy smirked and raised an eyebrow. I continued, "Butts are mostly used for practical purposes. Now a nice tush, on the other hand, can be fantastic, but as great as they are can leave an advanced student like myself wanting. An ass however is an amazing thing, a thing of beauty, a thing to behold and to be held." I closed the distance between us and took her hands in mine. "You, baby, have an *ass*."

Lucy's face flushed as I pulled her in for a kiss, which she quickly broke by playfully hitting my chest. "Hey! Are you saying I have a big butt?"

"No, Lucy, I'm saying you have the most amazing ass I've ever seen." I kissed her again, as my hands made their way to her perfect ass. She moaned as I pulled her closer, my hands right where I wanted them. Lucy squeezed her arms around my waist and my already hardening cock came to full attention. I was losing my mind. I wanted to tear every stitch of her clothing off, I could barely think of anything other than burying myself deep inside of her. Out of all of this, one thought became abundantly clear; I didn't know if I'd be able to last the weekend without fucking Lucy Haddon.

"Lucy, we have to stop now or I won't be able to." I tried to sound commanding, as I gently pushed her away, but even I didn't believe the words coming out of my mouth.

"Bam, I don't want to stop."

"Do you think *I* want to stop?" I asked. "We have to stop because we agreed that sex was off the table."

"We can still make out, remember?" she reminded me, sounding a little frustrated.

"Baby, if we keep making out like this, I'm gonna have no choice but to throw you down on that big ol' cow hide couch over there and do a variety of unspeakable things to you."

Lucy bit her lip and shifted her weight to one side in a pouty motion. Fuck me, did this woman know how *not* to be sexy? Here I am trying to do the right thing while the most beautiful woman on the planet is pouting at me. At this point, I was half hoping Sully would leap up from behind the couch with his, undoubtedly pearl-handled 9mm and put me out of my misery.

"How about you pour us a drink, and I'll get that fire started? We can sit right down on "ol' Bessie" and continue our conversation from earlier. Where do you store your wood?"

"Oh, there's a remote control there on that end table. Press the button marked "fireplace" on it." Lucy motioned to a small white touch pad and headed out of the room.

"Push a button? That's your idea of me starting a fire? Not very manly."

"Welcome to the new age, Captain Caveman," Lucy shouted from the kitchen. "Hey, speaking of stone-aged cartoon characters, what kind name is Bam Bam for a grown man? Wasn't that the Flintstone's baby?"

"Actually, Pebbles was the offspring of Fred and Wilma Flintstone and Bam Bam was the adopted son of their neighbors, the Rubbles."

"Well, I stand corrected."

"And so you should. However, I didn't get my nickname from the cartoon. My mom started calling me Bam Bam when I was five years old."

Lucy sat down next to me on the couch and set two glasses of red wine in front of us. "Is this okay?"

"I'm not much of a wine guy. Not much experience with it, actually, but I'll happily drink gasoline as long as you are here with me."

"No more smooth talk, Mr. Nelson," she warned, and sipped her wine. "Why Bam Bam?"

"Well, I used to take out all the pots and pans from the lower cupboard and beat on 'em with wooden spoons. I'd pretty much beat on anything remotely drum shaped. One day, I moved the day's drum solo over to her new coffee table and dented the shit out of it. We didn't have many nice things, and my old man had just bought a new living room set for my mom, most likely out of guilt from his latest affair. He saw what I'd done and was ready to beat the shit out of me for it, but my mom stepped in. She just grabbed me and laughed it off in order to cool him down. She said she liked it better this way, because I had turned an ordinary coffee table into art through my music. That's the way my mother saw things. She said it was "obvious that little 'Bam Bam' here was a drummer," and when the time came a few years later, she helped me buy my first drum kit."

"It sounds like your mother loved you very much," Lucy said, obviously fighting back tears.

"Anyway, from that day forward, she called me, Bam Bam. Pretty soon that's what everyone called me."

"Even your father?"

"*My father*? No way. He barely spoke to me and when he did he'd just call me 'hey you' or 'dick-head.'" Lucy dropped her head in an obvious attempt to hide her discomfort. "Hey it's okay," I said lifting her chin. "Where I come from, everyone's daddy is an alcoholic asshole, it doesn't make me special or anything." I tried to lighten the mood. I couldn't stand to see Lucy upset, and the fact that my father was somehow causing her pain made me hate him even more.

"He sounds like a monster. I can't imagine having that kind of relationship with my father."

"I didn't have any relationship with him." I chuckled.

Lucy didn't.

"I'm really sorry you didn't have a good relationship with your Dad, Bam. Even when things were at their worst in my family, all we wanted to do was be whole again—to be together. Dad's worked so hard to overcome his demons and regain our trust. Now that we've gone through what we have, and come out the other side even stronger, I can't imagine not having my father in my life. I can't imagine us being apart."

"I like that you have that," I said. "Right now, though, I can't imagine being away from you…being away from this place. You fascinate me."

"What could possibly be fascinating about me? You're the freaking rock star!" she protested.

"You're a badass, baby! For you to go through the kind of hell you did as a kid and accept your father back with open arms is amazing. You don't seem to carry around baggage or hold the past over his head. You're genuinely kind, but you don't take shit from anyone either. You seem kind of perfect actually."

"Believe me when I tell you that I'm far from perfect, Bam Bam Nelson." She sat up straight and set her wine glass down. "*Case in point*, what the hell am I doing here with you? I'm clearly horrible at my job. I'm supposed to be here as a vacation from work and to recharge before starting the next phase of work for the tour and here I am drinking and *canoodling* with the damned drummer of the opening band!"

"Canoodling? So we've finally defined what it is we're doing here?" I asked grinning.

"Stop being charming, Bam, I'm serious."

"I can tell. You have your serious face on; it's

your most adorable one." I kissed her quickly.

"I can't just let you keep charming me with your words and good looks, Bam." She sighed. "I don't want to screw this job up and I don't want to get hurt. I honestly don't know why I asked you here." Biting her lip, she rasped, "What am I'm doing? I've just met you and I'm letting you kiss me, call me baby, and grab my ass. You're probably used to women acting like this around you all the time, but this is not me. This isn't how I normally act."

I sat up and took her hands in mine. "I'm here to get to know you and to spend some time with you alone…that's all I want. I don't know why you're here, but I'm here for you. I don't want some groupie to fuck, and I'm not looking to fill anyone's rock star fantasies. I'm here for you."

I leaned in for another kiss, gently biting her bottom lip. Lucy shuddered and moaned as she stroked my neck. I deepened the kiss, but she surprised me by pushing me onto my back and straddling me on the oversized sofa. We continued to kiss as my hands began to explore her body. I cupped her full breasts, still fully hidden behind her sweater, and felt her nipples tighten.

She groaned and sat up, gently arching her back, my hands still firmly on her breasts—her hands now on top of mine—and rocked her denim-clad pussy against my denim-clad (and extremely hard) cock. Licking her lips, she turned her head slowly to the side and then let out a shriek.

"Sully!"

*** *** ***

Lucy

I flopped onto Bam's chest and scrambled off the sofa as he sat up slowly and faced Sully.

"What are you doing here?" I snapped.

"I knocked, Miss Haddon. You didn't answer. The door was unlocked, so I decided I should make sure no funny business was going on." Sully crossed his arms and glared at Bam. "It would appear I arrived just in time."

My face burned with embarrassment, but I squared my shoulders. "Sully, none of this is your business. You're supposed to be here in case I need you. You're not my father."

His head turned toward me and I didn't miss the expression of hurt on his face.

"What I mean is that I'm an adult," I corrected.

"I'm aware of what you meant, Miss Haddon." He turned his back. "I wanted to let you know there's a storm coming in, so please make sure you lock everything up tight and stay away from the windows."

"Okay, Sully, thank you." I glanced at Bam who gave me a bolstering smile. "Would you like to stay here?"

"No, Miss Haddon, I'm fine where I am. Call me if you need me." He walked out the door without a backward glance and I flopped down next to Bam again.

"I'm such a bitch."

Bam wrapped his arm around me and pulled me close. "You're not a bitch, baby."

"Sully's my favorite person in the world. I shouldn't have spoken to him like that."

"You were caught off-guard. I'm sure he understands."

"I should apologize." I tried to stand, but Bam kept me next to him.

"You can apologize tomorrow. Do you hear the wind?"

I did, unfortunately, which would keep me locked in the house for a while. "I'll lock up."

"I'll help you."

I nodded and led him around the house making sure everything was secure.

Lucy

T HE NEXT MORNING, I awoke to the smell of bacon and sat up with a gasp. If Bam was cooking bacon, he'd probably make it the way he had it in the diner and I'd have to insult his cooking.

I didn't want to insult him this early in our relationship.

I scrambled out of bed and stalled.

Ohmigod, I just acknowledged we're in a relationship. Shit.

I shook my head and made my way to the bathroom. Peeking out the window, I saw the storm from the night before had blown over, but the waves were still pretty choppy. After taking a quick shower, I dressed in yoga pants and a T-shirt, then met Bam in the kitchen.

Holy crap on a stick, he was adorable. He'd found one of my mom's aprons, a very floral one, and wore it, along with the matching oven mitt, which he had on as he pulled a baking sheet out of the oven.

"Mornin', baby," he said with a grin.

"Hi. I can't believe you're cooking."

"I love to cook," he said. "How do you like your bacon?"

"Not crispy," I retorted, and he chuckled. "I really like it English-style."

"So, limp."

"Sure, we can go with limp."

He raised an eyebrow. "I hope to hell that's all you like limp."

I giggled. "Pasta's always better limp, but other than that, I'm good."

He grinned, leaning down to kiss me gently. "You look beautiful."

"Thank you. What are you making?"

"Bacon, scrambled eggs, hash browns, toast," he rattled off. "Wasn't sure which coffee to use, though. There's a shit ton to choose from."

I smiled. "I'll make that. Mom likes to have a variety, but I only like one."

I walked into our massive pantry and grabbed the coffee, then made a pot. While it brewed, I leaned against the counter and watched Bam work. "Do you cook a lot?"

He shook his head as he scrambled the eggs. "Not as much as I'd like to, but as soon as I saw this kitchen, I knew I'd have to."

I smiled. "I like that you made yourself comfortable."

"Yeah?"

I nodded. "The few friends I've brought up here tend to get really nervous and refuse to touch anything. Either that or they're rich little brats who want to be catered to."

"You don't like rich little brats, huh?"

"No." I sighed. "I'm well aware my brother and I were brought up with money, but I try not to take anything for granted. Mom and Dad have been really clear that we won't get all of their money when they die. We'll get some, but we have always known we have to make our own way. I had to apply and interview for this job, even though Dad and the band were the ones making the hiring decision."

"Yeah?"

"Yep. It was the hardest interview I've ever had, honestly. I was up against a couple of really great people. People with a lot more experience than me."

"You don't think he let you believe you might not get it?"

I let out a snort of derision. "Not even close. Seriously. I almost didn't get the job. In fact, they offered it to someone else, but she decided cornering Dad in a back room and attempting to remove his clothing was a way to advance her career. She was wrong."

"Shit, really?"

I nodded. "Yep. To make things worse, "She was fired during the early planning stages of the tour, so, naturally what had been normal band chaos became my real-time job interview. Come to find out, she *really* sucked at her job, so I had a mess to clean up on top of everything." I shrugged. "But now I have the manager job, so it all worked out in the end."

"Until you come work for me."

I rolled my eyes. "Never gonna happen, buddy."

He grinned. "We'll see."

"How do you like your coffee?" I asked, changing the subject.

"Black's good."

I nodded and made us both a cup. After taking a few sips of coffee, I grabbed plates and silverware, and Bam dished everything up. We ate in virtual silence, mostly because I couldn't speak. The boy could not only kiss, he could cook.

"Good?" he asked.

"Ohmigod, *so* good," I breathed out.

He chuckled. "I'm glad you like it."

"You cook like you play."

"How so?"

"You throw everything you have into it and it's perfect," I admitted.

"Fuck me, seriously?"

"Yes."

He grinned, leaning over to kiss me gently. "Best compliment I've ever received."

"That can't be true."

"Cutest, then."

I blushed. "You're very sweet."

"No, I'm really not."

I giggled. "Hate to burst your alpha-male bubble, but yes, you are."

"Alpha male, huh?"

"Well, both my dad and brother fit that description, so I should know."

Bam chuckled as he grabbed our plates and set them in the sink.

"Leave those," I ordered. "I'll clean up. You finish your coffee."

"You sure?"

"Very." I smiled. "Go sit out on the deck. It's always gorgeous in the morning."

"Okay." He leaned down to kiss my cheek, and walked out of the room.

* * *

Bam

Apart from the inclusion of Lucy's robot assassin surrogate dad, this beach trip was going better than I could have hoped. Lucy was opening up to me and I had somehow managed not to screw her brains out, although the day had just begun. Last night's teenage roll on the couch did little to calm the raging hard-on I was walking around with, but I knew I had to be smart and be safe, for both our sakes. I had to remember that we were leaving here Tuesday morning and that reality was waiting for me back in Alabama.

Lucy had been a distraction, a welcome one, admittedly, but I still had a lot to process. When I got back to Elwood, I'd have to figure out what we were going to do about Chas and the money he'd stolen from us. I also needed to determine exactly what Zeke's involvement was and who was going to manage the band. Not to mention, I hadn't even thought about the fact that I'd eventually have to meet and play in front of fucking RatHound. It wasn't until Lucy mentioned Jack Henry's wife's death that I'd even grappled with the thought of meeting my childhood hero—the very man who was the reason I was a drummer.

The back deck had a breathtaking view of Puget Sound, but I turned my chair to face the house. I sipped my coffee as I watched Lucy cleaning up in the kitchen through the sliding glass doors. As nice as the back deck view was it had nothing on Lucy Haddon. The more I looked at her, the more I wanted her. This little vacation of mine was eventually going to come to an end, but I was determined to make every moment with Lucy count.

"You know the view is a whole lot better when you actually point your chair toward the water," Lucy said as she walked through the sliding doors.

"Says who?" I challenged.

"Very funny, Mr. Charming Pants," she said as she moved toward me, coffee cup in hand.

"Mr. Charming Pants? Is that *really* what you're going with?"

"Yes, as matter fact, from now on that's all I'll call you."

"All right then." I leaned back in my chair and smirked. "From now on I'm calling you Bambi."

Lucy's eyes narrowed. "You wouldn't dare."

"And why not? The big brown doe eyes. The lightly freckled nose. Hell, you're a dead ringer for Bambi."

"Bambi was a *boy*!"

"It doesn't matter…Bambi it is," I said matter-of-factly.

"You call me that and I'll…I'll…"

"What? Sic Thumper on me? Oooooh, mad Bambi is even more adorable than regular Bambi."

Lucy sat down on my lap and started poking at my stomach with her free hand.

"C'mon now. Tickling isn't fair fighting. You better quit, woman. You're gonna spill your coffee on me."

"Promise me you won't call me that," she said in feeble attempt to sound stern in between fits of giggles.

"But Bam and Bambi has such a nice ring to it, don't you think? Our mash up name works perfectly. A hell of a lot better that Belucy," I continued to tease.

"Is that where we're at—the nickname stage? What next, matching sweaters? Do we need to *define the relationship* as well?" she challenged.

I sat up a little straighter. "In all honestly, I'd prefer if we didn't." My words came out in a more serious tone than I had intended.

"Bam, I didn't mean anything by that. I was joking—"

"No," I interrupted. "I know that. It was funny.

I'm sorry. I just meant that I don't want to define what we have. I simply want to be with you, whatever that means. We have enough people and things in the outside worlds to think about later. For now let's focus on being here together."

"That sounds like a plan. In the meantime we can think of better nicknames," she said before leaning down for a kiss.

* * *

Lucy

My kiss was meant to be sweet, but it quickly grew urgent and passionate…which didn't help keep us stay on track with our commitment to no sex. At least, it didn't keep *me* on track.

We only had until Tuesday, but I knew it would feel like forever, especially considering I was dying to rip his clothes off and lick his entire body, starting with this chest. Gah! I needed to take a cold shower or something. I kind of wish I'd brought my pocket rocket with me, but I had no idea I'd need it.

Stupid on my part. Next time I'd plan better.

Of course, if there was a next time, I'd probably hide his clothes so he was forced to walk around naked.

This thought sent me down a rabbit hole I needed to drag myself out of. Beau Nelson naked…lordy, that needed to happen sooner than later.

"Luce?"

"Hm?"

Bam chuckled. "Where'd you go?"

"Sorry, was admiring the view."

"You were staring at me."

"I'm aware, Bam."

He grinned, leaning over to kiss me again. "I like that, Bambi."

I wrinkled my nose. "Really?"

He dropped his head back and laughed. "Couldn't resist."

I nodded to his coffee cup. "Drink your coffee."

"Yes, ma'am."

We spent the rest of the morning watching the waves and I was pretty sure I napped between conversations, Bam putting me fully at ease.

Bam

TUESDAY CAME FAR too quickly, and I found myself dropped back at the hotel watching Lucy driving away with a sadness I hadn't expected. As I crossed the lobby of the hotel, I was greeted by Jeff, the perky-as-shit day manager. He let me know in his "most helpful" tone that it was well past my scheduled check out time and that all of my belongings were safely stored for my convenience. Apparently, the band had only been booked at the hotel through Sunday and I had forgotten to extend my stay before leaving for the beach house.

"Are you able to book me into another room?" I asked.

"I'm sorry, sir, the hotel is completely sold out. There's a conference in town."

"Hmm, okay, any suggestions on another place?"

"I'm sorry, sir, the city's essentially sold out. It's a large conference." He waved me toward the concierge desk. "Let me see if there's anything outside of the city."

"Thanks, Jeff," I said, and followed him. I spent several minutes standing at the desk while Jeff typed away on the computer. In the end, the closest hotel he could find was a Motel 6 almost thirty miles away. Not conducive to caring for a new relationship when one doesn't have a car.

"Thanks for checking." I handed Jeff a folded five dollar bill.

He then went to retrieve my bags as I dialed Lucy's number.

"Hi, Bam," she answered.

"Hey. Are you guys far away?"

"Not too far, we're in traffic. Did you forget something in the car?" Lucy asked.

"No, I sort of got kicked out of my hotel." I chuckled. "The manager tried to find something else…"

"But the conference is making it hard to find anything?"

I sighed. "Exactly."

"We need to turn around and go back to the hotel please," she said to Sully.

"No, I don't need you to do that," I countered. "I just need a recommendation on where to stay."

"If Jeff couldn't find something, I'd imagine there isn't anything. He's very helpful."

"No shit," I said with a chuckle.

"Okay, give me a few." I could hear the smile in her voice. "I'll make some calls and let you know what I come up with. Sit tight and we'll be right there."

"Thanks, baby."

I hung up and dragged my bag outside. The hotel was busy, and after my idyllic weekend, I needed some fresh air.

Sully's Town Car had barley stopped moving when Lucy swung the back door open.

"Hey, mister, I hear you're looking for a place to stay," she said playfully.

"Sure, but that back seat looks a little small for the two of us. I was hoping for something a little roomier."

"Get in. I've got somewhere special to take you."

Lucy and I held hands as we drove through downtown Seattle. She was silent for most of the drive, choosing to communicate most through a series of adorable grins. She looked like the canary that had eaten the cat. I had no idea where we were going, but I didn't care because it meant I got more time with my girl.

Twenty minutes later I was standing at the front door of a palatial mansion that looked like something from the Italian countryside.

"Welcome to my parents' house," Lucy said with

a triumphant smile on her face.

"Are you fuckin' kidding me?" I said in a low tone.

"What? You need a place to stay, they have plenty of room, and you were going to have to meet them at some point anyway—no time like the present." Lucy looked very pleased with herself.

"Lucy, this is the third time within a week I've worn these clothes. I've got a black eye and I just spent the weekend rolling around on a couch with you like a horny teenager. You really think *this* is the time to meet the folks?"

"Don't worry, just be yourself and they will love you. It'll be fine."

Oh yeah, no fucking problem, you're just about to meet a rock legend and you look like a rented sack of turds.

Lucy opened the large front door, which was unlocked. We had driven through a private security gate on the way in, but I was still surprised at this. Where I come from, people don't have shit, but what little they do have is protected tooth and nail. I thought about the Haddon's hiring Sully and how seriously he took his job of protecting Lucy. People tend to protect what is most valuable to them.

"I don't think this is such a great idea. I can find a hotel… really," I argued while we stepped into the grand entry way.

"Don't be silly. I told you they have plenty of room."

"It's not the space I'm concerned about Lucy, I—"

I was interrupted by Roxie Haddon as she descended one side of the double staircase.

"Lucy girl, what are you doing here, everything okay?" Roxie was stunning. Her energy immediately filled the entire room and her welcoming smile immediately made me feel at ease.

What is it about these women that has such a calming effect on me?

"Like Dad didn't fill you in as soon as I hung up with him," Lucy droned sarcastically.

Roxie grinned and faced me. "You must be Bam, it's so nice to finally meet you,"

"Yes ma'am, thank you very much, it's a pleasure to meet you, Mrs. Haddon. I'm so sorry for the intrusion."

"Please, call me Roxie, and this is no intrusion at all. I hate that my baby girl lives so far away from me. Any reason to get her back here where she belongs is fine by me."

"Mom, I live ten minutes away!" Lucy said.

"See? Too far," Roxie retorted dryly.

"With no hotels open, Dad said Bam could stay in the guest house for a few days."

"Of course, we'd love to have you Bam. It'll give us a chance to get to know you better before the tour. We saw you play at the Gunnach Benefit and I could see why Lucy is such a big Roses for Anna fan."

I turned slowly to face Lucy whose cheeks had turned bright red.

"Is that a fact? A big Roses for Anna fan, hm? I'm not sure Lucy has mentioned that."

"*Mom,*" Lucy growled.

"What? I didn't know it was some sort of secret. I

just figured with all the posters on your wall when you were younger, that you would have told him you were a fan."

I couldn't figure out if Roxie was really innocent or stirring the pot. Apparently, the mother/daughter resemblance extended be-yond their good looks.

"Posters?" I gasped with mock surprise. "You had my poster on your wall?"

"One poster! I had *one* Roses for Anna Poster."

"Plus the one of Bam…shirtless…against the brick wall," Roxie added.

"Mom!" The volume and pitch of Lucy's voice apparently caught the attention of Rex Haddon.

"What are you two fighting about now?" he asked grinning as he walked down the stairs.

I tried not to stare, but I could do little else. Although in his early fifties, he looked like he was ready to kick ass and take names. I suddenly realized that, very, very soon, I'd be sharing a stage with this man. I would get to watch RatHound from the side of the stage every night. The fifteen-year-old kid inside of me freaked out.

"Please tell mom to stop," Lucy pleaded with her father.

Rex shrugged. "She's never listened to me before; I don't know what makes you think she'd start today."

Lucy glared at her father before replacing her expression with a gentle smile. "Bam, this is my father, Rex. Dad, this is Bam."

"Of course. How are you Bam? It's nice to meet you."

I shook his hand but wasn't exactly overcome with peace like I had been with the Haddon women. Don't get me wrong, Rex was friendly enough, but he clearly wasn't "impressed" with me. I was well aware that any charm I might possess would not work on him. Not that I wanted to charm him or his family. In the same way that I felt a need to fully reveal myself to Lucy, I felt a need to be very honest with the Haddon family.

"I'm fine thanks…doing great actually… it's… a real honor to meet you sir. Thank you so much for this…ah… opportunity." Words were starting to lose meaning as they fell from my mouth.

Pull it together, shithead.

"We're really looking forward to the tour, and please, call me Rex. Are you hungry? I was just going to make us a little something to eat."

Keep your cool.

"Um…no thank you, sir…ah…*Rex*," I stammered. "I'd love to be able to clean up somewhere, maybe do a load of laundry."

"Of course," Roxie said. "Lucy, sweetie, why don't you give Bam a tour of the guest house and show him where he can put his dirty clothes."

"Oh, I don't mind washing them myself Ma'am—*Roxie*."

"Wow, Rex could learn a few things from you Bam, *and* Lucy girl over there as well." Roxie motioned playfully toward Lucy who did nothing to defend herself.

"Lucy Haddon. Am I to infer, from your mother's comment, that you do not do your own laundry?"

"It's not like I *couldn't*," she answered defensively.

"Wait just a minute. I thought you *hated* spoiled kids."

"*Spoiled*, who said I was spoiled? I just happen to like the way my mother washes and folds the best."

"She washes *and* folds for you? No, that's not right. That's not right at all."

"I don't mind." Roxie smiled. "My personal laundry service gets her and her brother to come by the house more often."

I looked at Lucy sternly and wagged a finger at her. "Not right one bit."

She grabbed my finger and bent it a little painfully while keeping a serene smile on her face. "Come on, Mr. Shit Stirrer, please allow me to show you to your quarters."

Bam

GRABBED MY oversized duffle bag that I'd lived out of most of my adult life, and followed Lucy. She led me through a pair of French doors, past the pool and spa (shit, they had a pool *and* a spa), and to the "guesthouse." She pushed open the door and I glanced around the huge great room.

"This is the guesthouse?"

"Yeah, why?"

"It's bigger than most regular homes where I come from."

"Oh, you can thank Mom for that. We have crazy

relatives and she wanted to make sure it was big enough to accommodate enough people so she could limit her contact with her mother." She giggled. "According to Grandma, the pool house was far too small for her."

"Fuck me, you have a pool house?"

"Yes, Bam…we have a *pool*."

She said this like I was an idiot and should have known. Like every home with a pool was required by law to have a pool house.

"My bad."

She grinned and led me down the hall. There were three bedrooms, one the size of the doublewide I lived in until I was twelve, with four bunks on each side of the room, with its own bathroom and a huge closet.

The next bedroom was normal sized, but still had its own bathroom. The master bedroom was another story altogether.

"I thought you'd feel most comfortable in this room," Lucy said with a grin, swinging the double doors open.

The room was massive, furnished with a king-sized bed, oversized dark stained furniture, and steamer trunks that looked like they'd been used on actual African safaris. There were gold and platinum albums on the walls, and Grammys and MTV music video awards on display throughout the room.

On one side of the room was the iconic, all-black piano that Rex played in the video for "Song for Steven," which was the band's first number one song. Above it hung a large framed print of RatHound playing together on stage, shot from John Henry's perspective behind the drum kit. As spectacular as these sights were, my gaze quickly became locked on the back left corner of the suite. Behind another set of French doors (open to take advantage of the light) there was a spacious living area adjacent to the sleeping area that contained a bay window with a stunning view of lake Washington.

"Holy shit. Is that…" I couldn't even finish the sentence.

"Welcome to the Jack Henry Suite," Lucy said.

In the corner was a two foot drum riser, and on that riser sat the drum kit used by RatHound's drummer on their earliest major tours. Jack Henry was hands down my favorite drummer of all time and this was my favorite drum kit. I had posters of Jack Henry playing this very kit on my walls as a kid. This was the kit he played on "Release the Hounds," which was the very first RatHound album I bought.

"Why is this here? What is this place?" I asked, still stunned.

"When Pam died twelve years ago, Jack was in a very bad place. She was the love of his life and he was lost for a long time. Mom and dad put this place together for him to come and stay. They wanted it to be a reminder for him of better times. Jack is like a little brother to my dad. He's the youngest member of the band and I think my dad's always been really protective of him. He stayed here for a long time and it's still his place of residence whenever he's in town…which is almost never nowadays."

"You expect me to sleep here?" I blurted out.

"Why not?"

"This is like holy ground Lucy. I can't sleep ten feet away from *these* drums, in *his* bed!"

"Don't be ridiculous, it's at least thirty feet."

He rolled his eyes. "I'm not sure you realize how much of a hero this man is to me. He's the reason I play drums. He's almost mythical to me. It's like asking a squire to sleep in King Arthur's bed, next to Excalibur!"

"Boys are silly," Lucy turned slowly and began walking away ignoring my protests. "C'mon you can clean up in here."

Lucy led me into the master bathroom which unsurprisingly looked like something out of a home design magazine. I noticed several pieces of very old looking luggage stacked in the corner, and an antique shaving kit displayed next to the sink.

"I'll show you the laundry room and then you can shower or whatever before dinner."

"*Dinner*. It's a bit early to be to be planning for dinner isn't it?"

"You don't know my dad. If he has guests, a menu is being planned as we speak. Special dinners are an all day occasion and my father looks for any opportunity to go big." Lucy smiled and led me down a short hallway to the laundry room. As we moved into the space, her scent hit me like a drug. Barely able to control myself, I dropped my bag and kissed her, slowly backing her up against the washer.

"What are you doing?" Lucy asked.

"I promised you I would show you how much fun

laundry can be," I said.

"But you're supposed to be getting cleaned up," she said, breathlessly in between kisses.

The feel of her full tits pressed against my chest drove me crazy.

"I'd rather get much dirtier." I grabbed the bottom of her shirt, pulled it up over her head, and tossed it to the floor. Lucy pulled me closer, deepening her kiss. My hands made my way to her bra clasp when Lucy stopped me.

"Not so fast." Lucy broke our kiss and pushed me backward. "You first," she said while holding her bra up. I thought I might explode right then and there.

I pulled my t-shirt off slowly and Lucy bit her lip, nodding in approval.

"Now you, baby," I instructed.

Lucy dropped her bra to the floor and I couldn't contain myself any longer. I closed the distance between us and greedily took a beaded nipple into my mouth. Lucy groaned as I gently sucked, working my tongue as her hands ran through the tangles of my hair. Her breathing quickened and I continued my exploration. I grabbed her hips and quickly lifted her onto the washer. This way, I had full access to her tits. She wrapped her legs around my ass and squeezed tighter as I gently pinched her nipples.

"Damn it," Lucy said and let out a soft chuckle.

"What is it?"

"This washer is brand new."

"Don't worry baby, I don't think we're in any danger of breaking it," I said before returning my attention to Lucy's body.

"No that's not it. I was kind of hoping this would be one of those shaky older models. We could have turned it on and had some fun," she said with a devilish grin.

"Well please allow me to be your own personal spin cycle," I said, unzipping her jeans. I peeled them off in one swift motion leaving Lucy wearing only her white cotton thong. I bent down, slid Lucy's ass closer to the edge of the washer, and slowly began removing her last remaining stitch of clothing.

"I want you so bad Bam but we can't—"

"I know, baby," I said as I slid my hands down her stomach, making my way to her thighs.

Lucy quietly gasped as I gently stroked her inner thighs, before quickly parting her legs. My mouth made its way to her sweet pussy and Lucy let out a full volume moan. Her thighs becoming hotter as my tongue teased her clit.

"Ohmigod, Bam, yes," Lucy panted as she grabbed my hair with both hands. I took one of her tits in my hand while I worked her clit with my other, and continued with my tongue while Lucy writhed in ecstasy.

"Please don't stop," Lucy begged.

I had no intention of stopping. I drove my tongue deeper and deeper still until I could feel her on the edge.

Lucy arched her back and held her breath as my hands slid underneath her. I squeezed her ass as I drove my tongue inside of her one last time. She pulled my face closer to her as her thighs tightened and locked. I didn't care if I lost oxygen and passed out. Hell, I didn't care if I died. In fact, making Lucy Haddon come was all I could see caring about for the foreseeable future…and come she did. I lapped at her until she relaxed, then I stood and turned to exit the room.

"Hey, where are you going?" Lucy asked sitting up quickly and crossing her legs.

"I'm grabbing my bag from the hallway. I still need to do my laundry."

Lucy laughed. "Well, you took care of me—don't I need to take care of you?"

"You sure don't," I said matter-of-factly.

"Well, what if I very much *want* to take care of you?" she asked raising an eyebrow.

"Then you're going to have to wait."

"Wait, what? What guy doesn't want a blow job, and exactly how is this fair?" Her tone was a bit more serious now.

"Baby, if I allow you to suck my cock, I'll have to fuck you. It's that simple."

I could see Lucy's thighs tighten involuntarily and she bit her lip.

I continued, "We agreed that we weren't going to have sex, so I'm going to stop us right here, while we can. I'm going to start a load of laundry if you need to freshen up before we head back to the house. I'm going to do the same.

I took Lucy's hand and she hopped off the washer. I handed her her clothes and she headed off to the master bath wearing a somewhat puzzled expression.

We finished cleaning ourselves up, locked up our private retreat, and made our way back toward the main palace. Per usual, Lucy walked a few paces in front of me, so I hooked the back pockets of her jeans, stopping her dead in her tracks. I pulled her backwards, wrapped my arms around her and kissed her neck.

"Stop it, you jerk, they're going to see us!" Lucy wriggled away, fighting back laughter.

"Kissing's nothing. Wait 'til they find out what we just did in the guest house."

"You'd better not!" Lucy warned, smacking my chest.

"Better not what? Go down on you again?"

"You most certainly *will* do that again. That was amazing."

"Amazing, huh?"

"Honestly, I've never really done that before," she said somewhat sheepishly.

"*Really?*"

"No," she said in a hushed tone. "There were a few attempts by my boyfriend, but I always felt weird. I don't know, it was different with you somehow. I trusted you. I wanted you to."

"Thanks, baby," I said, wearing my best pussy eating grin.

We made our way into the main house via the rear entrance, which led into the kitchen. Rex Haddon was also entering the room via the opposite door with a large red and white envelope.

"What's that, Dad?" Lucy asked, trying to sound casual.

"I don't know, a courier just dropped this off," Rex said as he tore into the envelope.

My heart sank as the contents of the envelope were placed on the kitchen island. An advanced copy of SPIN magazine's latest issue was at the top of the stack, featuring yours truly splayed out on the floor, half dazed, complete with the headline: "RAZING HELL WITH ROCK'S NUMBER ONE BAD BOY."

Also within the contents were several other tabloid magazines and screen shots from various web media outlets. As I feared, the cell phone camera footage of my fight with Chas had hit the web and now I had to eat shit in front of my hero and his daughter, who I had just nearly fucked.

"Rex, I—"

"Roxie, we're grilling tonight!" Rex yelled as he scooped up the stack of magazines and papers. "Come with me Bam." Rex motioned to the back door and I followed him.

I glanced back at Lucy who gave me a silent, but exaggerated shrug. Was he taking me out back to shoot me? Or worse, maybe he was kicking us off the tour. I couldn't blame him either way. I'm sure this was not the kind of shit he wanted to deal with right now.

"I want to show you my favorite part of the house, Bam," Rex said calmly as we walked down a stone path toward a state of the art outdoor kitchen that overlooked the lake. The outdoor space was unbelievable, outfitted with a huge stainless steel grill, a full bar, flat screen TVs and a huge stone fire pit located in the center of a sunken lounge area.

"Check out the fire pit." Rex casually walked to the large flagstone circle and tossed the stack of articles on top of the ceramic logs. He then silently walked over to the bar, located a small red button which he pushed, igniting the gas, and sending the stack of smut papers back to hell.

Rex looked at me squarely and said, "I want you to know I don't give a shit about any of that stuff, Bam. The media, the tabloids, none of it. I've been there myself and I'd never judge a man based on what the media says. What I *do* care about is my family, my band, and my sobriety."

"Rex, I understand—"

"You don't understand shit yet." Rex paused and looked at me very seriously. "You're on top right now with no wife, no family, and not a care in the world. It's all glory and pussy for the foreseeable future and I understand the excitement surrounding that, but I need to know if you can keep your crew and your shit together out there."

"I can and I will, sir, I promise."

"Good, because I've been a big fan since Lucy turned me onto you guys."

"Lucy turned you onto us?"

"Yeah," Rex confirmed. "Not that I had much of a choice. Lucy was nineteen and living at home when your first album came out. She listened to it *a lot*. Very loudly. On repeat. I got to know your songs through the walls at first and then I started asking

Lucy to crack her door a little so I could hear more. Then I saw you guys play and I knew instantly that you were there real deal."

"I, I have no idea what to say," I stammered.

"I've treated you with respect, so you can tell me you'll take this tour seriously and that you won't endanger the things that are important to me—my family, my band, my sobriety"—He paused and lowered his head, his eyes locked on mine— "my *daughter*."

"Sir, I respect you and I really appreciate this opportunity, and the last thing I want to do—"

Rex waved his hand and turned away dismissively. "Ahhh, bullshit."

I must have looked crushed by the way Rex looked at me.

"Wait, that's not what I meant." Rex gave me a half-reassuring smile. "I believe that you're sincere, but that's not what I want to hear from you. I want to be reassured that you understand what's at stake for me and my family, and that you won't hurt my daughter who is clearly enamored with you. I want a hell of a lot more for her than to run off with a musician. "

"Rex," I said clearing my throat. "I really care about Lucy, but we've just started to get to know each other and we're trying very hard to not let our personal lives interfere with—"

"You see, that's exactly what I'm talking about." Rex said.

"I don't follow. I *really* do care about Lucy…and the tour and your family."

"You care, but you don't fully understand the

stakes yet. You don't understand the toll the road takes on a family. It's a beast that devours everything it can."

"Rex, I've lived out on the road all of my life, and I've seen the beast. I know the beast all too well."

"Maybe so, but I can tell by the look in your eye that you still think you can somehow control the beast— that you can tame it. You think that you're somehow strong enough to shield those that you care about from the damage it does. Well, let me tell you, my friend, you aren't, and you're headed for big trouble if you think otherwise."

"Then why the fuck am I here? If you don't think I'm ready, and you don't trust me around your daughter, why am I here?"

"You're here for two reasons. Lucy trusts you and I trust Lucy. Her judgment is almost always dead on. Her taste in music and in people is almost never off the mark." Rex studied me for a moment. "I'll be honest with you, Bam."

What the fuck have you been with me so far?

"You're also here because I see something in you as well. Lucy clearly thinks highly of you and that means a lot to me, but I'm serious when I say that I need you to have my back."

"I do, one hundred percent," I reassured him.

"Good. Oh, and of course if you hurt my daughter, even in the slightest of ways, your band will be shy a drummer and your road crew will be missing a flight case."

Great chat.

Lucy

I FROWNED AS **Dad** ushered Bam out to the grill. My body still thrummed with desire from our earlier make-out session. Good lord, the man's body was better than ever.

My mother's hand appeared in front of me as she snapped her fingers. "Luce!"

"What?" I asked, leaning my head away.

"Thinking back to the sex tape?"

"What? No!" I ground out. "Ew."

"Ew?"

"Yes, 'ew.' Melody's a skinny ho bag."

Mom chuckled. "She is a bit skinny, I agree. But

Bam—"

"Stop." I raised my hand. "Do not tell me you've seen the video."

"Have you?" she asked.

"I…it's a bit before my time, wouldn't you say?"

"That's not an answer, Lucy."

"Nope, you're right, it's not." I grabbed a bottle of wine and busied myself opening it.

"I'll show you mine if you show me yours," Mom teased.

I wrinkled my nose.

"Same time. Yes or no," she continued. "On three."

I sighed. "Fine."

"One, two, three…"

"Yes," I said, as she said, "Hell, yeah."

I groaned. "Ohmigod, Mom, you *watched* it?"

She got a weird grin on her face. "More than once."

I stuck my fingers in my ears and chanted, "La, la, la, I'm not listening."

She shrugged and poured us each a glass of wine.

"You watched it, honey," she pointed out. "You can't judge me for doing the same."

"*You're* married."

"Dad knew what I was doing. He even glanced at it…sort of."

I gasped. "That's even *worse*."

"Full disclosure," she corrected. "He wasn't that interested. He doesn't find Melody all that pretty and he wasn't interested in seeing 'another man's dick.' His loss I say."

I groaned. "No, Mom. Just…no."

"Well, Bam has a very nice penis. You'll have fun with that."

"Mom!" I squealed. "Stop talking."

"Nice, tight sac."

"For the love of *God,* Mother, do not say another word."

"I really like a man with a tight sac," she continued. "I was never a big fan of saggy balls."

I rushed to the sink and pretended to be vomiting into it.

Mom laughed so hard she bent over at the waist and I straightened, crossing my arms and waiting for her to laugh herself out… or choke. Choking would be good right about now.

"You should see your face," she said, still laughing.

"Are you done?" I asked.

"Nope." She held her hands out in cupped fashion. "Balls should be smaller than this…and Bam's are perfect."

"Stop." I rolled my eyes. "Ohmigod, there is something seriously wrong with you."

"You got rubbers?" she asked. "You'll need the extra-large ones…maybe ribbed for her pleasure."

"This is child abuse."

"Would you rather I not discuss this openly, honestly, and lovingly with you?"

"Yes, yes, I would."

"Too bad," she retorted, and her laughing began again.

"You know I get to decide what kind of home

you end up in, right?" I reminded her just as Bam and Dad walked back into the kitchen. I felt the heat burn uncomfortably on my face and busied myself in the fridge. I wasn't looking for anything, but it helped cool me down.

"Everything okay, Rox?" Dad asked.

"Oh, everything's great, baby," she said. "I was simply helping Lucy out with a personal issue."

"And now she's done," I said, closing the fridge a little harder than I meant to. "*Right*, Mom?"

Mom snorted, but managed to nod. "Yep. We're all good."

"Great. I'll grab the steaks, you grab the potato salad, yeah?" Dad said.

Mom nodded and followed him back out the way they came, leaving me alone with Bam, still crimson and feeling way too insecure for my liking.

"You okay?" Bam asked.

"Nope."

He frowned. "What's wrong?"

"Oh, nothing."

"When your mom said personal issue, I—"

"Nothing to worry about." I shook my head. "She was being obnoxious at my expense."

"Don't like that, baby."

I sighed. "I don't really either, but it wasn't malicious. Just her weird way of looking out for me."

He closed the distance between us and stroked my cheek. "You want to share?"

"Maybe when we know each other a little bit better, okay?"

He chuckled. "Okay, baby. I get it." He kissed

me gently, which didn't really help me calm down. "I'm starving."

I nodded. "Me too."

We grabbed drinks and a couple of sides, and headed out to where my parents were setting up. Mom and Dad were laughing and I had a feeling Mom had just added to my personal hell and shared everything with Dad.

"How do you like your steak, Bam?" Dad asked.

"Medium rare is great," he answered.

Dad turned to my mom. "How about you, baby? Do you still like your meat high and tight?"

"State geriatric ward for both of you," I snapped. "Not one single frill, I swear to God."

* * *

Bam

My phone buzzed right as I took my last bite of food. It was Mack. "Excuse me," I said to the family. "I need to take this."

"Go ahead," Lucy said, and I walked toward the water and answered the call.

"Hey, Bam, do you have some time to talk?" Mack sounded concerned.

"Sure thing," I answered. I suppose I should have been anticipating Mack's call since the Dogs of Fire were babysitting Chas for me. "Everything okay with Chas? Were you able to find anything out?"

"That's sorta why I'm calling," Mack said. "You asked me to poke around for any information about your money." He paused. "Good news, bad news on that. The good news is that I reached out to a contact in the FBI named Jaxon Quinn, and he knows where some of it is. The bad news is you'll have to go through the FBI to get it as it's now evidence in an ongoing FBI investigation."

"Fuck me. You've got to be kidding me."

"Sorry, brother, I wish I was. Apparently, Chas Chambers has been in business with some Dixie Mafia members for some time now. The FBI wants him because he's got intimate knowledge of their accounting system and has been stealing from them…exactly like he was from you. Once Jaxon knew we had Chas it was game over. The feds came and grabbed Chas and I wasn't about to jam up Jaxon by letting our guys stand in the way."

"I get it," I said. "I don't even give a shit about the money right now I just want that prick to pay."

"Don't worry, brother, he will. As for getting even, let me assure you that Chas will walk with a limp for the rest of his life—a life that will likely be lived out in the witness protection, once the feds extract every piece of cheese they can from that rat. At best, he'll live out the rest of his days in some Cleveland suburb under the name Larry Butts."

"Thanks, man." I chuckled. "Keep me posted."

"Will do, but that's not all I'm calling about," Mack said, the concern returning to his voice. "When Jaxon was digging around for clues on the whereabouts of your money he stumbled upon your mother's murder case. He became interested when he saw that it was unsolved, and even more so when he noticed local law enforcement had done virtually nothing to solve it."

"What?" I asked stunned.

"He said that it looked like the case ran cold quickly and was shelved as soon as it possibly could be even though very little investigating had ever been done. He'd like to meet with you in Elwood as soon as possible to talk about the case."

"I'm still in Seattle, Mack. I don't even know when I'm going back to Alabama. Besides, I haven't been back to Elwood in years."

"Well you'd better get there…preferably by Friday. Jaxon wants to start interviewing potential witnesses right away."

"Why would he want to do that? Why the hell would this guy care so much about my mother's unsolved murder case? "

"No clue. He just asked me to relay the message and to give you his number. Call him, Bam, Jaxon's a good guy. The Dogs trust him and I trust him."

Mack texted me the contact information for Special Agent Jaxon Quinn of the FBI.

Who the fuck spells Jaxon with an X? You already have a Q in your name, are you working the triple word score here?

"Thanks again, Mack, for everything. I'll give this guy call."

We hung up and I instantly hit Hadley's icon on my phone. Apparently, I was going to need a plane ticket home and I wasn't even quite sure why yet. The past few days with Lucy had been so amazing I hadn't even thought much about when I'd be leaving to go back to Alabama and now I was going back to Elwood of all places?

Lucy.

How was I going to tell Lucy I was leaving? Wait. How was I actually going to leave her?

* * *

Lucy

Bam took his phone call and then seemed to shut down. When I reached over and squeezed his thigh, he moved away from my touch and I was left wondering what the hell happened during his phone call.

Bam excused himself early and headed into the guest house, which meant I either had to tell my parents I was staying or head back to my apartment. Dad escaped to his "den," while Mom and I took care of the dishes.

"You okay?" Mom asked.

"Yep."

She raised an eyebrow but didn't press. "Are you going to stay?"

"I wasn't, but I don't want to make Sully come back," I said. "So, yes, if you don't mind, I'll stay."

Mom rolled her eyes. "If I could get you to move back home, I'd be ecstatic, baby girl, so I don't mind at all."

I smiled. "You're ridiculous."

She pulled me in for a hug. "Just love my girl."

"Love you too, Mama."

"I'm going to find your dad. Lock up, okay?"

"I will," I promised, and took a couple of the kitchen towels into the laundry. The laundry room was at the back of the house and gave me a direct line of sight to the guest house. It looked as though the great room light was on, and I debated heading over. I desperately wanted to see Bam, but with his coldness toward me earlier, I wasn't sure it would be a good idea.

But…I'd had a couple glasses of wine, so I decided it was enough liquid courage to find out what the hell was going on. After setting the alarm, I locked up and walked to the guest house.

Knocking on the door, I was forced to wait for several minutes, and actually almost left before the door was pulled open with surprising force.

"Yeah, Had, that'd be great," Bam said, and waved me in. "Nothin' yet. Just gotta sort that shit out first. Yeah, we can talk then. Okay. Yep. Yep. Thanks."

He hung up and faced me. "You okay?"

I nodded. "I'm kind of wondering the same thing about you."

"Just sorting out some band business. I have to head back to Alabama tomorrow."

"I thought you were going to stick around a bit."

"Can't. Gotta get home." He headed toward the kitchen and I followed.

"What's going on, Bam?"

"Just got shit to deal with."

"Can I help?"

He grabbed a bottled water out of the fridge and faced me again. "No."

"What's going on?"

He took a sip of water but didn't answer my

question.

"Bam."

"It's all good, Lucy. Don't worry about it."

"You're shutting me out."

"Can't shut you out when it doesn't have anything to do with you."

Direct hit.

I shoved my emotions deep down and nodded. "Got it. I'll see you whenever."

I stalked toward the front door, but before I reached the foyer, I found myself pushed up against the wall and kissed like I was Bam's lifeline.

"Fuck!" he snapped as he broke the kiss.

"Last chance to tell me what's going on, buddy," I warned.

He dragged his hands down his face.

"I'm leaving."

He grabbed my arm gently. "Wait."

"Why?"

"Baby, I don't want any of this shit to touch you."

"Too late." I crossed my arms. "If we're entering into a relationship, you need to fill me in on what's going on. I'm not the kind of girl who's okay with being kept in the dark."

"And I'm not the kind of man who'll let drama touch my woman."

"Well, I'm not truly your woman if you're not willing to share the good *and* the bad."

He shook his head. "Baby, this isn't something you share with the woman you want to keep. I tell you all this shit and you'll fuckin' run."

This statement filled in another piece of the puzzle that was Beau "Bam" Nelson and I wrapped my arms around him. "Did you kill someone?"

"No."

"Did you hurt someone? Cheat on someone, rape someone, steal from someone?"

"What the hell? No, baby. Nothing like that."

"Okay, then I'm not going to run."

"I don't want to burden you."

I rolled my eyes. "I'm asking you to. You don't have to face all of this alone anymore."

"I honestly don't know all of the information. Just that the FBI has been digging into my mom's murder."

"Why would they do that?"

"No clue, but I have to be back in Elwood by Friday."

"Wow," I whispered. "Are you okay?"

He shrugged. "I don't know."

"This is going to hit you hard when you get home."

"Probably."

"Do you want me to come with you?"

"There's nothin' I'd like more," he said. "But I really don't want this to touch you. I'll deal with it."

I hugged him tight. "If you need me, I'll come."

"Thanks, baby. I appreciate it."

"When's your flight?"

"Seven a.m."

I met his eyes. "There wasn't anything later?"

"Not direct, no."

"You could take the band jet."

"There's a band jet?"

I nodded. "I can talk to Dad—"

"No."

"He won't mind—"

"No," he interrupted again. "I need to deal with this without getting your dad involved, Luce."

"More alpha male philosophies?"

He chuckled without mirth. "Sure. We'll go with that."

"Let me have Sully drive you to the airport."

"I'll grab a cab or an Uber."

"*Or* I can have Sully drive you. And if you don't mind, I'll ride with you."

Bam smiled…finally. "I'd like that."

"I'll let you go," I said. "You should probably try to sleep."

"*Or* you could stay."

"I could. This is true," I said, smiling up at him. "And if I stay, what will we do?"

"Anything you want."

"Really? Anything?"

"Yeah, baby, anything."

"I kind of want to get naked."

"Yeah?"

I nodded, heat creeping up my neck. I had *never* been this forward in my life. "Will you think less of me?"

"Why the hell would I think less of you?"

"Because we've barely met and I'm standing here offering myself up to you."

He dropped his head back and laughed. "Holy

shit, you're adorable."

I frowned. "Excuse me?"

"Let me fill you in on a little secret." He took my hand and led me to the overstuffed chair facing the fireplace, tugging me onto his lap. "Unlike my band mates, I don't get off fucking every woman who offers herself to me."

"Um…" I squirmed, very uncomfortable with this conversation. I wasn't really interested in hearing how many women had offered themselves up to Bam. I was pretty sure it was millions.

"Stay with me, Lucy. Just hear me out, okay?"

I sighed, but nodded.

"I'm a one woman kind of guy. I only sleep with women I'm in a relationship with. I don't cheat and I don't lie. My last relationship was with Melody and you can understand why it's been a while since I've been with anyone."

"Well, since I don't really know why you broke up, I don't know that I *can* understand."

"It was in all the tabloids."

"I don't read the tabloids, Bam. It's gossip and I hate gossip."

"I like that about you." He stroked my face and kissed me gently. "It was a messy break up. She cheated with her ex, Jason Maxx."

"The country singer?"

"Yeah. They've been off and on since she was sixteen. He's got a hold on her that she can't seem to shake and I got caught in the middle of their drama."

"I'm sorry, Bam."

"It's *so* not a problem," he said. "I was committed to her, but I was never really in love with her, so it didn't hurt nearly as much as the media made it out."

"So you're over her."

"So fucking over her, Luce. I was over her before *we* were even over if that makes sense."

"When did you guys make the sex tape?"

"Fuck me, have you seen it?"

I nodded. "So have my parents."

He dropped his head back with a groan. "Shit."

I giggled. "It's nothing for *you* to be embarrassed about."

"It is what it is," he said, although his tone was somewhat irritated. "We made it together, so I couldn't say I didn't know I was being filmed, but we'd talked about deleting it after watching it. Melody felt she needed a way to kill her squeaky clean image and "leaked" it. I was pissed. It was the final nail in the coffin of our shitty relationship."

"Can we make a pact never to make a sex tape?"

Bam chuckled. "Yeah, baby. No problem."

"I'd really like to have sex, though," I whispered.

"I can make that happen," he whispered back. "But…"

"But, what?"

"We do this, and we're in it. You're mine. I'm yours. We work our shit out."

"Fair warning, I can be a little jealous."

"Same, baby. But I don't cheat."

"Neither do I," I said. "I'd either dump you or kill you and hide your body before I'd ever cheat."

He chuckled. "Good to know."

I kissed him and he stood, lifting me with him, and carried me toward the bedroom. My heart raced knowing this was finally going to happen.

Lucy

AM DROPPED ME gently onto the mattress. I slid my hands into his hair as he stretched out beside me and proceeded to remove my clothes slowly…painfully slowly. He drew a nipple into his mouth and bit down gently. I arched into his mouth as he continued to shower attention on my breasts while sliding a hand under the waistband of my panties and between my legs. His finger slid through the wetness and then slipped inside of me. I groaned and pushed against him as he slid another inside. His thumb found my clit and I moaned. I could feel my orgasm building, but before it washed over me, he removed his hand.

"Don't stop," I demanded as he stood. "Where are you going?"

He pushed his jeans from his hips and I grinned. God, he was magnificent. After he slipped my panties down my legs, he slid on a condom and rose up above me, settling his hips between mine and guiding himself inside of me. I wrapped my legs around him and arched up.

"Fuck, baby." He slid out of me and then back in slowly. "God, you feel so good."

"Yes," I whispered.

He covered my mouth with his and thrust deep inside of me.

His tongue slid into my mouth as his cock surged deeper and deeper, faster and faster. "Bam!" I cried out.

I felt my orgasm build and relished the feeling, but when his hand slid between us and his finger found my clit, it was over and I exploded around him. I gripped his biceps and tried to catch my breath. Within seconds, I felt Bam's cock pulsate inside of me and he chuckled as he rolled us onto our sides. "I feel like a fuckin' teenager."

I giggled. "Why?"

"Because I had to come," he admitted. "I'll make that last next time."

"I quite enjoyed that, so if you can make it last longer, I'll probably enjoy it even more." I kissed the top of his head and grinned. "I hope you have a *lot* of condoms."

His body stilled. "Yeah, baby. I have enough." He smiled and kissed me before sliding out of me and heading to the bathroom.

He returned and stood at the edge of the bed wrapping his hands around my thighs. "You on the pill?"

I leaned up on my elbows. "Yes."

"Still gonna use protection until I can show you I'm clean." He pulled my body down the bed, causing me to fall onto my back again, and sliding my legs over his shoulders.

"Okay," I whispered.

I shifted as his mouth kissed his way down the inside of my left thigh. He gripped both of mine and found my eyes. "Don't move. Get me?"

I took a deep breath and bit my lip, dropping my head back to the mattress. He lowered his mouth to my clit and sucked until I couldn't help myself from bucking my hips. He gripped my thighs tighter and lowered my bottom to the bed, spreading my knees. I whimpered as he sucked harder, slipping a finger inside of me. Without warning, he stood, pulling me further down the bed, and slammed into me. I cried out and arched again.

"Too much?" he asked.

"God, no. Harder," I demanded.

He grasped my thighs again, holding them against his hips and lifting me slightly as he surged into me. I fisted my hands in the comforter, somewhat unable to do much else because I was anchored to his body. He thrust into me again and again, his body locked as he held me to him. I cried out as I came around him, but didn't have time to enjoy it as I was flipped onto my stomach and taken from behind.

I steadied myself on all fours and Bam reached around me to cup my breasts. His movements were slower now, which only managed to drive me crazy. "You okay?"

I pressed back into him. "Yes."

He squeezed my leg gently. "Wider, baby."

I widened my legs immediately and his hand left my breast and found my clit. I groaned, grinding against him. He slid in slowly again and I sighed. "More, Bam."

"Patience, baby."

I reached between us as he slid out of me again and wrapped my hand around his cock. "No. I want you to fuck me."

He pushed into my hand and I released him. He hissed. "Fuck."

Bam took the hint and slammed into me again and I cried out in relief. His thrusts came harder until I exploded around him and my face hit the mattress, then he surged in two more times and I felt his cock pulse as he came inside of me. "Mine," he growled.

"Yes," I whispered.

He kissed my lower back and then my bottom, before sliding out of me and heading to the bathroom to get rid of the condom.

* * *

Bam

I climbed back onto the bed, leaning over to kiss Lucy. I knew I should probably go slow and give her time to adjust, but my dick had other ideas. I had to have her again. She was mine. This thought rocked me to my core because I'd never felt that way before. I had never been a fuck you and leave you kinda guy, but even in my previous relationships, I'd never felt a connection this strong. Lucy was quickly becoming everything to me and I needed to figure out how to keep her from leaving me.

"Hey," she whispered, stroking my cheek. "Where'd you go?"

I shook off my fears and smiled. "Nowhere, baby. I'm right here."

My attraction to her had always been more than just physical, and I burned for her at every level, but right now I needed to connect with her physically more than I'd ever needed anything before.

"I'm here and I need you again."

"Well lucky for you, I'm right here."

"Yes, but I want to be *here*." I slid my hand to her pussy, cupping her mound.

"Don't tease me," she groaned.

"Baby, I don't want to hurt you."

"How about you let me tell you what hurts me." She arched into my hand. "Now, how about you slide that cock inside of me…quick like."

"My pleasure," I said and obliged.

Lucy's nails dug into my back as she took in my full length. I started a slow steady rhythm, and she whispered, "Faster, Bam."

I continued my slow pace until I felt she couldn't take it anymore. I had her right on the edge, which is exactly where I wanted her.

"Ohmigod, Bam, harder."

I finally acquiesced and sped up, driving myself deeper and deeper. Lucy's hands grabbed my ass as I slammed into her and I almost came right then. I pulled out, rolled onto my back and pulled Lucy on top of me. She straddled me, giving me full access to her tits.

"I'm in fuckin' heaven," I said, sitting up and kissing her breasts. She pushed me back down and I entered her once again as she arched her back before steadily riding my cock, taking me in deeper and deeper.

"I'm going to come Bam."

"Not yet," I warned.

"I can't wait, please," she pleaded.

I lifted her slightly and tugged her down on my cock again

"Beau!" she screamed, and I came just as her orgasm hit.

We collapsed and lay together in silence for what felt like forever, our bodies still locked together.

"I could do that to you all day long," I whispered.

"Someday soon, I'm going to let you."

* * *

Lucy

The next morning, I awoke to soft lips on my shoulder. "No," I let out with a moan.

Bam chuckled. "I have to go."

"No, that was the nightingale bird thing you heard… not the lark. Right? Lark's are assholes and wake people way too early in the morning."

"Did you just try to quote Shakespeare to me?"

"Excuse me?" I admonished, and rolled to face him. "I believe I quoted that line warmly and accurately."

"I don't think Shakespeare used 'asshole' in reference to birds or other creatures."

"I didn't actually read anything he wrote," I admitted.

"No? Did you do one of the plays or something?"

I blushed and shook my head. "I watched the 60s movie…when I was twelve."

"Lucy Roxanne Haddon," he breathed out. "Did your parents know you were watching it?"

"No," I whispered. "And to be honest, I wasn't quite prepared to see boobs."

"Her tits were gorgeous."

"As tits go, sure," I said. "But his butt? Mmmm."

"Naughty minx." His hands landed on my sides and squeezed.

I squealed with laughter. "Bam!"

He rolled me onto my back and hovered over me. "Do you know how beautiful you are?"

I bit my lip and stroked his face. "Back atya."

"Do you know what it did to me when you screamed my name…my real name…when you came last night?"

I shook my head.

"Well, then I'm gonna need to show you."

Bam kissed me gently…sweetly. I heard the tearing of foil and he sat up briefly, then he slid slowly into me and I wrapped my legs around his waist. He linked his fingers with mine and dragged my arms above my head making it so I couldn't touch him. He released one of my hands, but I still couldn't move…he simply held me still with one hand while the other twisted a nipple into a hard pebble before sliding his fingers between us and working my clit.

"Beau," I whispered. "I can't wait."

"Now, baby."

I shattered and wrapped my arms around his neck when he finally released my hands. Bam kissed me again, got rid of the condom, then stretched out beside me and pulled me onto his chest. "I have to go."

I slid my hand up his stomach. "No."

He chuckled. "I *will* come back, baby."

"Not soon enough."

His phone beeped and he gave me a gentle squeeze. "I really need to go."

I rolled onto my back and sighed dramatically, dropping the back of my hand to my forehead. "Fine. Leave me. I'll just lie here and die of a broken heart."

His face appeared above me and I forced myself not to laugh. "You done?"

"Haven't even started," I quipped.

He grinned and kissed me quickly before climbing off the bed. "I'm gonna hit the shower. You comin'?"

"Do I get another orgasm?"

"Does a bear shit in the woods?"

"Probably. But hopefully he does it after an orgasm."

Bam laughed and I reluctantly climbed off the bed and joined him in the shower.

Bam

THE RED NEON glow of the Rudy's Place sign cast an ominous glow over the few cars left in the parking lot.

What the hell am I doing back to Elwood?

Most of us (me and the band) now lived in Montgomery, which is about seventy-five miles away from Elwood, but once I'd moved there I had yet to return to my hometown. There were simply too many ghosts there.

I grabbed my bag from the taxi's trunk and checked my watch. It was a little after midnight; still plenty of time before last call. I was definitely going to need a few drinks to get to sleep, but that wasn't the only reason for stopping in. Rudy's Place was one of the oldest bars in town. My good friend Tucker Harman's family had purchased the place when we were kids and he had been running the joint for years. I knew if I was going to start poking around town, I'd need to play a little catch up first. Who better to help me do that than the local bartender?

"You can't spell Alabama without B…A…Fuckin' M!" Tucker yelled from behind the bar, grinning widely.

"Mother Tucker!" I exclaimed back warmly.

Both the bar, and Tucker looked more or less the same as I'd last seen them. Perhaps both were a little worse for wear, but still full of character.

"What the hell is Mr. big time rock star doing here?" Tucker asked while coming from behind the bar, his arms held out wide.

"I keep asking myself the exact same thing brother," I said as we hugged. "I'm actually here to meet with an FBI agent about my mother's murder case."

"No shit?

I nodded. "We're meeting tomorrow, but I wanted to stop in here first."

"Drink?"

It was a point of pride among certain southern men to use as few words as possible when conversing. Tucker had always excelled at this.

"I'll take a Maker's Mark if you're pouring," I said.

"How long since you've been back home?"

The word *home* rattled around in my head for a while. I knew what he meant but it had been a long time since Elwood was home. I suppose Montgomery was *really* my home. It's where my place was, but I'm not sure it ever felt like home. In reality, the road had been my home since I was a kid. In the past ten years I'd slept more on busses and in motel rooms than anywhere. In fact, it had only been two years ago that we'd moved out of the band house and each member got his own place. Even though we'd finally started making some real money, I was still renting a place. It never felt quite right to put down roots there.

"Since right after my mother's murder," I responded.

"And now the FBI is looking into her case?"

"I guess so. Honestly, I'm not really sure what the fuck is going on, that's why I'm here."

"How can I help?" he asked with what I knew was genuine concern. People from Elwood wore their hearts on their sleeves, for better or worse. You always knew where you stood with the locals.

"Well, for starters you can pour me another one of these," I said as I finished my drink. Tucker smiled and happily obliged. "Next, you can tell me where I can find my old man."

Tucker stopped smiling. "Shit, Bam, you don't know? No one told you?"

"Told me what?" I asked slowly.

"Your father's dead, bud. He died about three years ago."

"How?"

"Cirrhosis," he answered plainly.

I hated my father and wasn't at all surprised to hear that he drank himself to death, but the news that he was dead still sent a shock through me. Regardless, I refused to allow myself to feel one ounce of pity for the man.

"Fuck him," I said as I raised my glass, before slamming down the remainder of its contents.

"He's still your daddy, Bam," Tucker said.

I shot him a look to remind him of what a prick that man had always been.

"Fair enough," he responded and poured us both another round before making a toast of his own. "To the return of the prodigal son and the death of his asshole daddy."

"I'll drink to that," I responded before bringing the sweet amber heat to my lips.

* * *

Lucy

My phone buzzed and I answered as soon as I read the screen. "Hey."

"Hey, baby," Bam rasped.

"What's wrong?"

He let out a sigh. "My dad's dead."

"Oh, honey, I'm so sorry."

"Don't be," he said. "He was a fuckin' piece of shit."

I bit my lip and blinked back tears. "Bam."

He sighed again. God, he sounded wrecked.

I leaned against the kitchen counter. "Can I just say something and then I'll drop the subject?"

165

"You'll drop it forever?" he challenged.

"If you want me to," I promised.

"I want you to."

I rolled my eyes. "I get that your dad wasn't a good man, but he still sort of helped to raise you. Even if you don't feel as though he did a good job, I happen to really like the man you've become. Despite the fact you probably did most of that yourself in spite of your father, it must be a mind bend to have lost the two people who made you. So, I would really love it if you'd let yourself grieve."

"Not sad he's dead, Luce."

"I get that, honey. But you need to let yourself feel whatever it is you're feeling. Don't stuff it, okay?"

He didn't say anything for several tense seconds. "I hear you."

"Good." I smiled. "I'm here if you need me."

"Got it."

"Dropping the subject now," I said.

"Appreciate it, baby."

"Are you sleeping?"

"As much as I did before."

I wrinkled my nose. "Will you promise me you'll take it easy?"

He chuckled. "Right."

"Well, will you promise me you'll *try* to take it easy, then?"

"Yeah, Lucy, I'll try."

"What's the plan tomorrow?"

"Meetin' with the FBI guy, then I guess I'll go

from there.”

“Are you nervous?”

“Kind of, I guess. Just wish this shit would die, you know?”

“I do, honey. I’m sorry.”

“Not your fault.”

“I know, but I wish I could be there with you.”

“I’m gonna finish it as fast as I can.”

“That’d be good,” I said.

“Oh yeah? How come?”

“No reason…I just miss you.”

“You do?”

I lowered myself onto the sofa. “Um, duh. You gave me, like, forty-two orgasms last night.”

He chuckled. “You want me for my dick…I get it.”

“Well, excuse me for wanting a little bam bam from Bam,” I retorted. “My rabbit simply doesn’t suffice anymore.”

“Better fuckin’ not,” he warned. “Your orgasms belong to me now.”

“Well, then you better get back here quick-like. I need more.”

“I’m workin’ on it.”

“Where are you staying?”

“Shithole motel at the edge of Elwood.”

I giggled. “How many motels *are* there in El-wood?”

“Just one…which is why I’m here.”

I shuddered. “Ugh, nothing better, huh?”

“Not unless I want to spend most of my time in the car,” he said. “It’s fine for the moment. As soon as I’m done, I’ll be heading back to Montgomery so

I can wrap shit up with the band."

"I wish I was there," I said again. I was admittedly fishing, but he hadn't said the magic words before.

"Me too, baby."

There they were. I grinned.

"I'm gonna let you go," he said. "I'll call you as soon as I can tomorrow."

"Okay." I stood and walked into the kitchen. "Talk to you tomorrow."

"Bye, baby."

"Bye."

We hung up and I put my plan into motion.

* * *

Bam

I stepped out into the morning air and dialed Jimmy's number.

"Hey man, what's going on? What time is it?" he answered.

"Early," I responded with a smile. It was always good to hear Jimmy's voice.

"Why the fuck are you awake during commuter sheep hours? I thought you were on vacation."

"I'm home actually. That's why I'm calling."

"Shit, man, if you're home, swing by a little later when I'm awake."

Jimmy and I lived four doors down from one another.

"I'm not at my place, I'm home, as in *down home*."

"You're in Elwood?" Jimmy responded, now

sounding a little more awake.

"Yeah, I won't be in town for long, but wanted to let you know I was here in case you heard something from the family."

"What brought you back to Elwood?"

"My mom," I answered. "The FBI is looking into her case and I'm meeting with a guy this morning. He wants to poke around and figures I can help."

"Wow, you want me to come down?"

"Thanks man, I'm good. Honestly, I'm not even exactly sure why I'm here, but I figure if there's a chance we can finally find out who's responsible for my mother's murder I have to do everything I can."

"Let me know if there's anything I can do."

"If you could let the guys know what's going on, I'd appreciate it," I said. "I should be back in Montgomery in a few days and we can talk then."

We wrapped up our conversation just as I reached the Starlight Diner. I pushed through the double doors, the familiar smell of coffee, stale cigarette smoke, and breakfast on the griddle momentarily transporting me back in time. I couldn't recount the hours I'd spent in this diner.

I noticed a stern looking man in a dark blue suit sitting with his back against a wall, eyes on the exits, and since he looked totally out of place, I assumed this was Agent Quinn. I made my way to the table and gave him a nod. "Agent Quinn?"

"Mr. Nelson. Nice to meet you," he said, shaking my hand as I sat down.

"Please call me Bam."

"Bam. Thanks for meeting with me so early. I

know you got in late last night, but I'm on a bit of time crunch and so wanted to get started as soon as possible."

"What's all this about exactly?" I asked impatiently.

"Simply put, I believe your mother's murder may somehow be linked to an ongoing FBI investigation into the Dixie Mafia. I would have never found the possible connection had Mack not asked me to look into your stolen money."

Special Agent Jaxon Quinn seemed like he was all business. He looked totally out of place in this small town diner and yet completely confident. I had no idea if this guy was going to be a straight shooter or full of shit, but Mack asked me to trust him, so that's what I was going to do.

"Chas Chambers has serious ties to the Dixie Mafia," he continued. "They bankrolled his earliest business ventures when he arrived here from England twenty years ago. He proved to be a capable earner for them, and knew how to handle himself when things got rough. It wasn't long before he was known as trustworthy within the organization, and not much long after that he started skimming from them."

"I'd love to say I'm shocked," I said flatly.

"You knew about his ties to the Dixie Mafia?"

"No, but I'm not surprised that piece of shit is involved with them. It wasn't my choice to bring him on. I never liked the guy and I hope he rots in the shittiest federal prison there is, but I still don't see what any of this has to do with my mother."

"Upon looking for the money Chas had stolen from your band, I saw that we already had a file on him due to his mafia connections. Your name was in his file due to him being Roses for Anna's manager, which isn't strange, but I did notice a flag on your name."

"What do you mean a flag?"

"You were listed as potential witness in your mother's murder case and the recorded statement you gave to the police was attached."

"Why does the FBI have a file on my mother's case? Wouldn't that all have been handled by the local police?"

"Yes, but about a year ago the bureau noticed a pattern of unsolved murders throughout Alabama, Louisiana, Arkansas, and Mississippi, that appeared to date back over fifteen years. The killings were identical, and all in Dixie Mafia territory. Once I saw the details of your mother's murder, and how little the local PD did to solve it, I knew we had another example."

"Example of *what* exactly?"

"Of a Dixie Mafia hit."

Lights flickered behind my eyes and my field of vision narrowed. I took a deep breath to keep from blacking out. "A hit? Why would my mother have been executed by the mafia?"

"All I can tell you right now, is we're building a case against some key players. I have some big questions and there may be people within this town that can provide answers."

"I don't know anything and have barely spoken to anyone in this town since I left. I can't see how I can be any help to you."

"People in this town know you, Bam, and I have a feeling they will talk to you a lot sooner and easier than they would talk to me."

"Maybe. But if people didn't talk twelve years ago, why would they talk now?" I asked.

"Because… I'm the one asking the questions this time," he said in a low, controlled tone.

Well, shit.

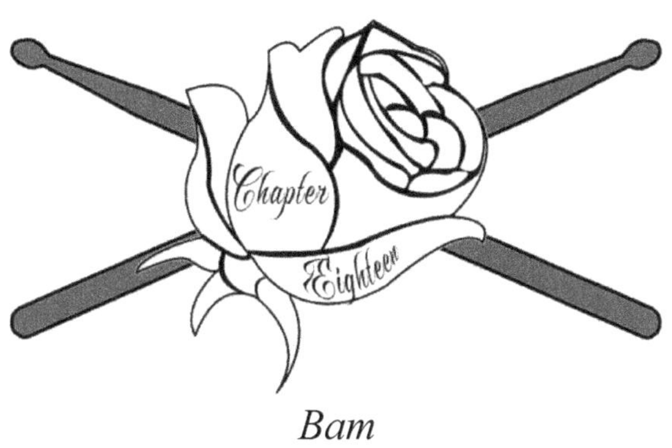

Bam

AS JAXON AND I made our way down Main Street, I tried to wrap my mind around everything I'd learned so far. The morning's heavy dose of caffeine coursed through my veins, but still, I was more tired than I'd ever been. Every thought that wasn't about my mother's case or Elwood was reserved for Lucy. I wished I hadn't told her not to come. Even though I didn't want my past to interfere with our relationship, I also didn't want this distance to interfere with our future together. I simply couldn't get her out of my head.

We moved toward the office of Dr. Wayne

Greene, who was not only one of the town's most beloved family physicians, but he'd also served as the county medical examiner up until a few years ago. He'd been the man who'd delivered me, and the same man who had to perform my mother's autopsy. He was the first person of interest on Jaxon's list and I wasn't looking forward to this visit. I knew I'd have to relive her death all over again once I'd agreed to help start digging into her case again, but knowing we'd be talking to Dr. Greene made all of this somehow feel even more real.

"What kind of information are you hoping the doctor will provide?" I asked.

Dr. Green's office was located in the oldest part of town, in a converted historic home, as were many of the local businesses. Elwood was a town of only a few thousand people, many of which had ties to this community well before the Civil War. Things moved slowly here and changed at an even slower pace.

"I'm looking for any and all information that is not in his official report," Jaxon answered. "The report I have gives little detail about her injuries and there's what looks to me like an inconstancy regarding her time of death."

We reached the office and entered. Behind the front desk was an elderly woman that must have been well into her eighties.

"Good morning, may I help you?" she asked pleasantly.

"Yes ma'am. We have an appointment with Dr. Greene. I'm special agent Quinn and this is—"

"Beau Nelson, is that you?"

As soon as she spoke my name I realized who she

was. Miss Bunny was our school nurse when we were kids, and had patched me up more than any other student in history according to her. I was constantly getting into fights, falling from high places that I shouldn't have been, and jumping my BMX bike off of homemade ramps that were made from pallet scraps.

"Miss Bunny, you look as beautiful as ever," I said smiling.

"And you look like you've been fighting again, young man." Her frail index finger pointed toward the faint remains of my bruised eye.

"I'm afraid I'm guilty as charged ma'am," I said sheepishly, then tried to change the subject. "You're working for the doc now, huh?"

"I've been his assistant for almost ten years…since my retirement."

"So you didn't work for Dr. Greene at the time of Anna Nelson's death?" Jaxon asked.

"No, I was still the nurse at the elementary school at the time, but of course I remember that awful ordeal. That poor dear, she was so young and beautiful. Her death was such a shock to all of us in Elwood, and of course my heart broke for little Beau."

She looked at me with a sadness that instantly reminded me of why I left. The final blow up with my father was what had ultimately convinced me to leave, but, if I were being honest, I had one foot out of town already. After my mother's death, I couldn't stand to have people look at me with pity in their eyes. I didn't want to be viewed as some sort of wounded bird or victim. I couldn't even stand to hear the sound of my own name once my mother was gone, so I left, shed as much of the past as I could, and never looked back.

Just then, Dr. Green appeared, welcomed us, and invited his into his office. Much like the rest of Elwood and its citizens, he was exactly as I remembered him, only a little older. He was a round man with a bright pink face and a stark white mustache. He'd always worn a bow tie and spoke in a deep rich baritone southern drawl.

"Tell me, gentlemen. What can I do for the Federal Bureau of Investigation and for our local celebrity here?" he asked jovially.

"I'm investigating the murder of Anna Nelson and would like to ask you a few questions regarding your autopsy report," Jaxon said.

"Oh my, well, 2005 was some time ago," Dr. Greene replied sounding somewhat evasive.

"I understand that it's been a while, but anything you might remember about the case would be really helpful to us," Jaxon said as he handed a file folder to Dr. Greene, who opened it and examined the contents carefully.

"Well, it sure looks like this report is in order. My notes are as I remember them, and everything looks correct to me. I didn't have anything more to add then, and I'm afraid I don't have anything to add now." He looked up at me. "I'm sorry, son, I'm not sure I can help you."

"I think you can, Dr. Greene," Jaxon said. "Perhaps you recall something that *wasn't* in your report."

"How is that exactly? Everything I know is in my original report, which I've just told you, looks good to me."

Jaxon crossed his arms and stared pointedly at the doctor. "I find that fascinating, because your report seems vague, incomplete, and possibly inaccurate."

"Inaccurate?" Dr. Greene's pink face took on a beet red hue. "I'll have you know, I was this county's medical examiner for twenty-five years and no one here has ever questioned my findings on a case or accused me of misconduct."

Jaxon paused. "I never said anything about misconduct doctor, only that your report is lacking details and quite possibly full of mistakes. *Unless...* they aren't mistakes at all. Are you covering something up, Dr. Greene?"

He sputtered with indignation. "I don't have time for this, I have patients to see—"

"Dr. Greene, why does your report list the time of death at approximately 9:00 p.m.?" Jaxon continued unfazed.

"Because that's when she died. Now I really must ask you gentlemen to leave, I have nothing more to say on this matter."

Jaxon pulled out a small notepad from his pocket and his fingers scanned one of its pages. "The body Anna Nelson was found at a little after 10:00 p.m. by a man named...ah, here it is...Grady Jones after he noticed his dogs barking at something in his field. Is that correct?"

"Yes, but—"

Jaxon ignored him and carried on with his questioning, "Then please explain to me how her body was in full rigor if she had only been dead for about an hour. Rigor mortis takes at least three to six hours to fully set in, which would've placed her actual time of death somewhere between 4:00 p.m. and 7:00 p.m. According to phone records, Mr. Nelson spoke with his mother for the last time at 4:19 p.m., so that narrows the timeline down a bit. Given when they last spoke, the state of the victim's body, and the remote location where she was found, I'd calculate the time of death window to be closer to 5:00 p.m. to 7:00 p.m., and certainly well before 9:00 p.m."

"Well, it's a good thing that you're not a medical examiner, young man. Now, if you'll please excuse me—"

"One more thing, doctor, then we'll leave you to your patients, although I don't recall seeing any in your waiting room when we came in."

Dr. Greene shifted in his seat.

"Why does your report list the cause of death as a single gunshot wound to the back of the head?"

"I don't understand the question," Dr. Greene replied. "I wrote that in the report because, that's how she died; a single gunshot to the back of the head."

"Then why were there two bullet holes?"

I felt my blood run cold. What the hell was he talking about? It had always been reported that my mother was shot once, likely in a carjacking gone wrong. I turned to face Jaxon but his gaze was fixed on the doctor, who had now risen to his feet.

"I must ask you both to leave right now or I'm going to call the sheriff. You have my final report and I've told you I don't know anything else. I won't stand here and have you lob accusations at me and my quality of work." He turned to face me. "I'm sorry about your mama, Beau, and about your daddy, I really tried to help him—"

"I don't give a shit about the last days of my father," I snapped. "If you have information about my mother's murder and you are holding out on us, this town is going to have another homicide on its hands." I took one step toward the doctor and Jaxon stepped in front of me.

"That'll be all for now, Dr. Greene," Jaxon said. "Thank you for your time. We'll be in touch soon." Jaxon ushered me out of the office and through the empty lobby, past a very concerned looking Miss Bunny.

"What the fuck are you doing?" I protested as we made our way out the front door. "You said yourself that he's lying, or at least covering something up. Why aren't we in there grilling him more?"

"Patience, Bam, you can only push someone so far. Besides, now he knows we're onto something and will likely reach out to whoever else is involved. This could be a way for us to start flushing the others out of hiding."

"Whoever else is involved? You actually think this is some sort of conspiracy? That my mother's death had something to do with the Dixie Mafia and that Dr. Greene covered it up?"

"Actually Bam, that's exactly what I think."

* * *

The next few days were the worst trip down memory lane I could imagine. Jaxon and I interviewed what felt like half the town, but made little progress. The people of Elwood were friendly but very guarded. Most folks around here didn't trust outsiders or the government, and so were reluctant to speak with Jaxon. Sometimes my presence helped and sometimes it backfired. Some people felt that I had "big timed" them by leaving and becoming successful, and some treated me like a rock star. I didn't know which was worse. Most people simply didn't want to talk about my mother's murder, or acted like they didn't know what we were talking about.

"We've been at this for several days and have come up with jack-shit," I said as we pulled onto the private road that led to the Jones farm.

This was to be the last interview of the day and the one I had been dreading the most. Grady Jones had found my mother's body in his back field and called the police right away. At first he was very helpful, but became very tight lipped after just a few days into the investigation. Then the investigation came to a grinding halt, and the case was put on the back burner as a possible "robbery motivated homicide."

"I know it's tough Bam, but try to be patient," he responded.

"Patient? It's been twelve years? How much longer does my mother have to wait for justice?

180

What the fuck are we doing here? These people probably won't want to talk to us anymore than anyone else in town. We're spinning our wheels and wasting time."

"I'm on your side, Bam, and believe it or not, we *are* making progress."

"Progress? How do you figure?"

"Dr. Greene is clearly hiding something, and I get the general feeling from the locals that the folks in town are afraid."

I rubbed my forehead, warding off a headache. "Afraid of what? The Dixie Mafia? You still haven't told me why you think my mother would be involved with them, or why they would have killed her."

"There are things I can't tell you yet, and there are details I'm still trying to bring into focus before I say anything definitively. This is our last stop, so let's see what we can find here and go from there," he said reassuringly.

The Jones place was a small soybean farm on the edge of town. Honestly, I was surprised it was still up and running, as it was on the verge of failure when I had left. Not only had the farm not failed, but it appeared to be thriving. The main house, barn, and equipment all seemed to be in tip top shape, and the size of the crop acreage had increased noticeably.

"I thought you said this place was a dump," Jaxon said as we walked toward the front porch.

"It was back in the day, believe me. As kids we'd tear through these fields and raise all sorts of hell. There was little more than dirt and rusted out pickup trucks around here."

Jaxon nodded toward the south field. "Looks like Mr. Jones's fortune has changed for the better while you've been away."

"Indeed," I replied softly as we reached the front porch. We didn't get any further when Grady Jones flew out of his front door holding a double barrel shotgun.

"I know why you boys are here and you can turn right back around," Grady said.

"Mr. Jones, we'd just like to ask you a few questions about—"

"You deaf? I told you I know why y'all are here, I don't care. I want you off my property." He raised his gun ever so slightly. "Now."

Jaxon sighed. "Mr. Jones, if you don't lower that weapon right now, I'm going to show you my gun. I'll also show you my shield and credentials, and then you can see the back of my shitty rental car. The next thing you'll see after that is the inside of an FBI black site cell, and trust me when I tell you, there is one closer to here than you'd think."

Grady lowered his gun, but kept the same shit sniffing expression on his face. He had always been a mean bastard, but this was more than typical grumpy old man bullshit.

"Thank you. Now, as I was saying, we'd like to have a chat with you and I promise we won't take up much of your time," Jaxon continued.

"You won't be taking up *any* of time. I told you I want you off my property and I meant it. You can talk to my lawyer if you want, but I got nothin' to tell you.”

“Thank you. That would be great,” he replied.

“What’s that now?” Grady asked.

“Your lawyer’s number. I’d love to get that from you.”

“The fuck you talkin’ about, boy?”

“You told me to talk to your lawyer, and I’m more than happy to do so, do you have his card?”

“Fuck you. His name is Harlan Caster, his office is in Montgomery, and he’s in the book. Now get gone.” He punctuated his statement by spitting into the dirt, mere inches from our feet. A long string of tobacco spittle clung to his chin.

“Thank you for your time sir,” Jaxon said, turned around and motioned for me to follow. We got back in the car and drove off.

“Why the hell didn’t you ask him any questions?” I asked. “Why did you let him off so easy?”

“Because I got exactly what I needed from him.”

Lucy

"**T**IME TO BUCKLE up," Sully announced over the loudspeaker.

I closed my laptop and smiled at Mary, who was my flight attendant for the day. I'd borrowed the band jet to surprise Bam, and booked me and Sully in at an historic bed and breakfast hotel in Montgomery. It was quite a distance from Bam's hometown, but I just couldn't stay in a dive motel that only charged twenty bucks a night. I shuddered at the thought. I knew it would probably be filthy and the bugs…ohmigod, the bugs in the south were bigger than most toddlers, so, ew…no. I couldn't do it. I needed a place with air-conditioning and clean bathrooms.

I really hoped Bam would be happy to see me. He'd sounded tired on the phone, which just didn't sit well with me. He was like the Energizer Bunny… always "on," but on the phone he'd sounded drained.

I sighed and shook off my worry. Instead of dwelling on the negative, it was time to put my plan in motion.

* * *

Bam

We pulled into the parking lot of Cumming's Motel which the locals called the Cum Motel due to the fact that the last letters of Cumming's had once burned out and stayed that way for several months before the owners bothered fixing it. After that, kids would chuck rocks at the sign to try to break those letters. Despite the motel's name and rough exterior, it proved an adequate enough place to hole up for a couple days while we grilled the locals.

The whole thing felt like a waste of time to me, but Jaxon was undeterred and actually seemed pleased with the results we were getting. I'd hoped we'd have some answers by now, but all I had was more questions.

"You've gotta let me know what you're thinking," I said to Jaxon as he parked.

"About what?"

"About all of this? Do you have a theory? Do you have any idea who actually killed her, or is this just a big fishing trip?"

"I told you, there's only so much I can tell you, and that you'll need to be patient."

"I get that, but we got chased away by a crazy old man with a shotgun. He didn't tell us jack shit and yet you seemed pleased as punch."

"He told us plenty."

"See, that's the shit I'm talking about!" I snapped.

"Bam, you're going to have to trust me. The puzzle pieces of this case are starting to come together, but the picture is much bigger than you think. There are a lot of agents working this case, and we have to be careful to preserve its integrity. The Dixie Mafia is no joke, and we have to be careful."

"Don't get me wrong, I don't mean to sound ungrateful, and I really appreciate you taking an interest in my mother's case—"

He stopped me. "It's not just an interest, Bam. I believe your mother's killing might be the piece of the puzzle we've been missing. I think I've got exactly what I needed from this trip and I'm flying back to the Portland office in the morning. I appreciate your help and will keep you posted on any new developments."

"Keep me posted? You've barely told me anything at all so far!" I exclaimed.

"I understand and I promise I'll get you up to speed as soon as it's appropriate."

I could tell Jaxon was being straight with me, but I wasn't happy. It was hard enough for me to tear this wound open again, but now he expected me to sit here bleeding? Fuck that.

"What the hell am I supposed to do while you're back in Portland?" I asked.

"Nothing. You do absolutely nothing. Go back home, get back to your life and I'll reach out to you when the time comes. I know you don't really know me, but I need you to trust me."

Since I couldn't speak without eviscerating him with my words, I gave him a curt nod. I knew that he was doing his best, and that I was being an asshole, but the weight of all of this on top of everything else that I was dealing with was starting to crush me. I needed to sleep. I needed to stop thinking, and most of all, I needed Lucy. I exited the car and leaned into the open passenger side window. "Call me as *soon* as you have something."

Jaxon nodded and pulled out of the driveway. As his tail lights faded into darkness I headed for the motel's main office. My head was pounding and I needed ice in order to make an icepack.

As I approached the office I could see the soft blue flicker of a TV screen inside, but no sign of the night manager. The light above the front door was off and the door was closed and locked. I rapped on the door a few times to no avail so I headed back to my room. The entire motel had an eerie calm about it and I found myself looking over my shoulder several times.

As I neared my motel room, my high alert status shot to code red. I could see light pouring into the walkway from my slightly ajar door. I closed and locked that door when I left, so the fact it was now open wasn't right.

I passed a large dumpster in the parking lot and grabbed the first potential weapon I could find; the board from a broken palate which had two nails sticking through one end.

The sound of footsteps behind me spurred me to walk faster, and I took a deep breath wildly swinging the door open as I raised my makeshift weapon over my head.

I heard a scream, just as my body was hit like a Mack truck from behind and thrown to the ground…my weapon landing nail side down…barely out of reach.

"Stop fightin'!" the familiar sound of Sully's voice growled in my ear.

"Sully?" I rasped, unable to fully expand my lungs with his knee in my back.

"Ohmigod, Bam?"

"Lucy! What the hell are you doing here?" I demanded.

"Apparently, I'm about to be murdered by a maniac with giant board," she retorted. "Sully, let him up."

"Is that an order?" Sully challenged.

"Stop being ornery, Sully," Lucy snapped. "Let him up."

I took a deep breath once Sully stood and pushed myself off the ground. Sully stood and I snapped to my feet, our faces now inches from one another.

"That one I can let slide, but if you ever put your hands on me again—"

"Bam!" Lucy admonished.

Sully scowled, his hands fisted at his sides.

"Let it go…both of you." She addressed us like we were kids fighting on the school yard. She grabbed my face and turned it toward her sharply. "Bam, tell me you understand."

I nodded slightly and let out a short grunt of acknowledgement.

"You too, Sully. As a matter of fact I want the both of you to put an end to your…your…penis measuring contest, or whatever this thing between you is."

Sully and I looked at each other, paused, and then started laughing. Hard.

"What's so funny?" Lucy demanded, but I was unable to respond. My lungs and stomach were on fire. I couldn't remember the last time I had laughed this hard.

"Goddamn it you're adorable," I wheezed out once I was able to compose myself.

"I am not! I'm serious. You both need to back off in the protection department. I can take care of myself. I also need the two of you to stop fighting over me and start getting along. You're both very important to me, but you're both being jackasses."

"You're right," I said smiling.

"Miss Haddon, I apologize," Sully said, now fully recovered and back to his factory settings.

Lucy cleared her throat and motioned toward my hand.

Taking the hint, I extended it to Sully. "No hard feelings, man."

Sully shook my hand, saying nothing but giving me a reassuring nod. With some men that's all it took. A handshake and a nod and we're good; it's just that simple. It's that way with good, honest men and I could tell Sully was a good man and that Lucy was like a daughter to him.

Sully finally broke his silence. "I'll be out in the car, Miss Haddon."

"Thank you, Sully," she said.

"What are you doing here?" I asked once again.

"You sounded so sad on the phone I thought I would surprise you."

"Well, I'm surprised. I think we were all surprised." I laughed.

"What the heck is going on here? Why did you charge through the door with a board like that?"

"I saw that my door was open and the lights were on. I thought maybe someone had broken in to my room."

She blushed. "I told the manager I was your girlfriend and wanted to surprise you, so he let me in."

I wrapped my arms around her and pulled her close. "You're not my girlfriend, Lucy."

Her body locked. "What?" she squeaked.

"You have girlfriends when you're sixteen, baby."

"Oh, really?"

I leaned down and kissed her. "My woman's more accurate, don't you think?"

She giggled placing her palms flat against my chest. "Your woman, huh?"

"Damn straight. You got a problem with that? 'Cause we might—"

She kissed me and her hands moved to the sides

of my head, her fingers sliding deep in the tangles of my hair. She broke the kiss and sighed. "I love being your woman."

* * *

Lucy

Bam kissed me again, his hand sliding under my shirt. As much as I couldn't wait to get naked, I wasn't prepared to do it in a dive motel.

"Wait, honey," I rasped, forcing myself to break the kiss.

"Seriously?"

I smiled, tapping his chest gently. "I can't get naked in a gross motel room. I just can't."

He chuckled. "What if I fuck you on the desk?"

"What if..." I licked my lips, "...we head into Montgomery and we make love in the really nice bed and breakfast room I have booked?"

He tugged one of my bra cups down and worked my nipple into a hard bead. "*Or*, I can fuck you up against the wall right now, *then* fuck you again in the bed and breakfast."

I leaned into his touch. "Bam," I whispered.

His hand moved to the waistband of my jeans. "Yeah, baby?"

"I—"

Bam's fingers slid under my panties and between my legs. "You, what?"

I swallowed and tried to catch my breath as he cupped my mound. "I—"

"Wall?"

"Ohmigod, yes, the wall," I managed to pant out.

191

I kicked my shoes off and Bam pushed my jeans and panties off my body, shoving me up against the wall and lifting me so I could wrap my legs around his waist.

He unbuckled his belt, unbuttoned his fly, and pushed his jeans low enough to free his cock. Before I could relish the sight of his gorgeous body, he slid into me and I whimpered with need.

Holding me steady, he pushed my shirt up so he could get access to my breasts. Since I didn't want to fall, all I could was grip his shoulders and hold on as he slammed into me over and over again. My orgasm washed over me and I screamed out his name, dropping my head back against the wall.

Bam gave my nipple one last suck, then kissed my neck and my lips before smiling and stroking my cheek. "Better?"

"So much better," I rasped. He pulled out of me and started to lower me to the ground. "No."

He chuckled. "You want more?"

"No…I mean, yes, but I really don't want my bare feet to touch the nasty floor."

He rolled his eyes and set me on the bed instead, handing me my discarded clothing before righting his own.

"I'm gonna pack real quick, then I'll drop my key in the dropbox and we can go."

"That sounds good," I said.

He grabbed a duffel and opened one of the dresser drawers. "You know, I have a place in Montgomery."

"You do?"

He nodded. "I haven't been there in a few weeks, but I know my cleaning lady came less than a week ago, so it can't be too bad."

"I can leave Sully at the B&B and we can go to your place if you like."

"Sounds good to me."

I waited while Bam finished packing, then he dropped the key at the front desk and we headed to Montgomery.

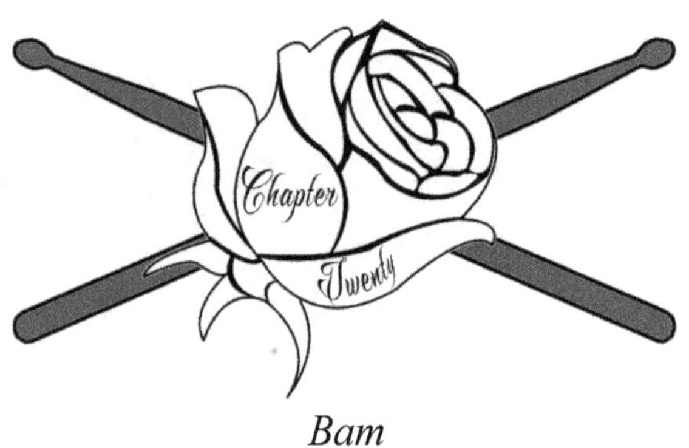

Bam

M Y PLACE WAS exactly how I left it. Dark, empty, and void of any and all life…but it was clean. I'd never realized just how depressing and uninviting my house was until the moment Lucy was standing in my living room.

"Well, here we are," I said.

"Charming," Lucy said playfully. "Does the glamor of your rock and roll lifestyle have no end?" she teased.

"Yeah, I sort of went with a minimalistic approach to the dé-cor.”

My building was about ten years old, and I’d been in my one-bedroom apartment almost four. Since I barely stayed here a week out of the month, I had the absolute necessities and nothing more.

Her eyes scanned the space. “That explains the overwhelming absence of furniture.”

“Ah, I see you have a sophisticated eye for design.”

“Bam, seriously! How long have you lived here? Did you even bother to unpack when you moved in?”

“This *is* unpacked. I guess it never really felt like home, so I never bothered trying to make it feel homey.”

“Forget homey, what about livable?”

“I have a couch, a TV, a bed, a fridge, and a kitchen island, what more do I need?”

“How about a fireplace or a source of heat?” Lucy suggested, rubbing her arms.

“Oh, you want a little heat in here?” I wrapped my arms around her and drew her in for a deep slow kiss.

“That *does* make everything a little better,” she replied.

“Come on. I’ll show you the bedroom.”

* * *

Lucy

Bam’s apartment was really sad. Not because of the fact it was a little run-down, I didn’t care about that, but because it wasn’t a home. A deep sense of sadness washed over me and I forced it back. He was alone… truly alone.

"What?" he asked, and brought me out of my thoughts.

"Sorry. I was just…"

"Tell me, Luce. I know this place is a dump and it's not what you're used—"

"Stop it," I hissed. "Your apartment is fine…it's just…"

"Just what?" he challenged, his body locked.

"It's lonely." He relaxed and I stared up at him. "I know we're new and there are never any guarantees in life, but you're part of me now…part of my family." I gripped the lapels of his jacket. "I never ever want you to be lonely again."

He smiled, stroking my cheek. "Being alone doesn't mean you're lonely."

"I know, but if you ever feel lonely, I want you to tell me."

"Yeah?"

I nodded. "Promise me."

He chuckled. "I promise, baby."

I kissed him quickly and then took in his bedroom. "This is a little more like it."

He had a king-sized bed (no headboard, but the bed was made), a dresser and a couple of nightstands, along with a nice sized bathroom with a door that led to the hallway and his room.

"Something I dropped some coin on was the bed. Can't sleep on a shitty mattress."

I grinned. "Me neither."

"And before you ask, no other woman's been in

this bed."

I relaxed and smiled. "I wasn't going to ask."

"Liar."

"Okay, I was thinking about it, but whether or not I was going to ask is another story."

"Now you don't have to ask." He kissed me gently. "And before you ask your other question…"

"What other question?"

"I have never had any women over…dating-wise."

I giggled. "So, mind reading is one of your abilities, huh?"

"Yep. Wanna know what you're thinking right now?"

"Do tell, oh wise one."

He lifted my T-shirt over my head and kissed my neck. "You want to get naked so your man will eat you out."

I shivered. "Ohmigod, that's amazing! It's exactly what I was thinking."

Bam chuckled, kissing me gently then we separated long enough to remove our clothes. I finished before him, so I had a chance to watch him undress. He was already rock hard. I licked my lips, suddenly wanting him in my mouth. I knelt in front of him, cradling his cock in my hand and kissing the tip. I took as much of him as I could in my mouth. God, he was big, but I pushed through and nearly choked with the girth of him.

"Luce," he whispered, pulling back slightly.

I ignored him and slid my mouth over the tip again, drawing him further into my mouth.

"Condom," he whispered.

"You didn't care about one earlier," I pointed out.

"Yeah, not my best moment."

I grinned taking him in my mouth again, pumping with one hand and cradling his balls with the other.

I knew I was giving him what he needed when he fisted his hands into my hair and his hips began to move. I couldn't stop a smile as he fucked my mouth, me a willing participant, holding on when he told me he was going to come. He warned me again, but I grabbed his ass and squeezed.

"Fuck!" he said with a groan as he came.

I waited until his cock stopped pulsing before giving one more suck and releasing him. I didn't have time for smug satisfaction as I was lifted and dropped back on the bed; my knees bent and Bam sliding into me slowly, but no less deliciously.

"Beau," I whispered.

He kissed me and his tongue swept against mine as he surged into me.

I arched my hips, drawing him further in. "Yes," I breathed out.

Guiding my hands above my head, Bam held them there with one hand, sliding his other to my breast. As he rolled my nipple between his fingers, he kissed me deeply, slamming into me over and over again.

I cried out his name as I came, trying to drag my hands from their prison to touch him, but he held firm and didn't release me until he came inside of me, eliciting yet another orgasm from me.

"You're fuckin' amazing," Bam breathed out, pulling me over his chest.

"Back atya." I kissed his chest and snuggled close. "I like no condoms…can we skip them from now on?"

"Not sure how I feel about that," he admitted. "Want to get tested first. I can do that tomorrow morning."

"I just figured we've done it twice now…"

He chuckled. "I'm clean, I know I'm clean, but you should be a little more concerned about your own well-being, baby."

I shrugged. "As weird as this sounds, I trust you."

"Love that, Luce."

I grinned, surprised by a sudden yawn. "Sorry. Traveling always wipes me out."

"It is late. Let's sleep and I'll take you to breakfast tomorrow before the band meeting."

I yawned again. "That sounds perfect."

He pulled the covers up around us and I let myself fall into oblivion.

* * *

Bam

Driving through town with Lucy by my side filled me with a strange sensation. Even though I had lived here for years, it was as if I was taking in my surroundings for the very first time. Her very presence made me look at my life from her perspective.

We were scheduled to meet the rest of the band at noon and we were running a little late due to the fact breakfast ran late. Truth be told, breakfast ran late because I spent an hour showing Lucy all the things I loved about her body.

The Sullynator had agreed to let me shuttle Lucy around today, but I had a feeling he wasn't far away. As we pulled into the back lot of the band's rehearsal space, I could see each band member's car. Everyone was here which meant, either the band was ready to work through our shit and get back to business, or I was walking into an ambush. I was prepared for either scenario.

"The Clubhouse" had been the band's official headquarters for the past five years. It was a converted machine shop in an old industrial area of town. It wasn't much to look at but it was secure, secluded, and so far had remained off the radar of the paparazzi.

We climbed out of my truck and Lucy stood staring up at the stark building.

"And for our next stop on this edition of Cribs," I joked.

"This is where you rehearse?" Lucy asked. "It looks more like where you'd split up the loot after a bank robbery."

I laughed. "I plead the fifth, but I'd watch what you say about the Clubhouse. I spend more time here than I do at home."

"After seeing your place, I can see why."

"Hey! My house isn't *that* bad," I challenged. "Perhaps it simply needs a woman's touch."

"Your house needs more than a woman's touch, it needs a bitch slap."

"You didn't say that when I bitch slapped your

ass this morning."

She bit her lip. "Your bed is amazing, as is your ability to make me come forty-two times in less than a minute."

"It's a gift." I leaned in for a kiss, but Lucy pulled back. "What's wrong?"

"I'm nervous," she said.

"About kissing? I think you should be over that by now, no?" I teased.

She rolled her eyes. "About seeing the band."

"Lucy, you've met the band."

"I know, but now I have to go in there as your girlfriend, or woman, or whatever. They'll probably look at me like a rookie manager with a crush, or a complication, or your side piece—"

"What the fuck? Baby, you're not a side piece and anyone who looks at you like you are will be picking up their teeth."

"Okay there, let's not get riled up. I'm just nervous. This is complicated for me. The band is your family and I want your family to like me. I also want to do a good job for *my* family, and to complicate everything you're right in the middle."

"I get that," I admitted. "The band has a lot of repair work to do before this tour starts, and I don't know how they're going to react to us being together, but you're not a complication Lucy, you're my lifeline. You are the only thing keeping me together."

I wrapped an arm around her waist and pulled her close, kissing her slowly. I took my time, knowing this would be the last time we'd be alone for a while.

She broke the kiss and grinned up at me. "That helps."

I chuckled. "Good."

I walked Lucy inside, but she dropped my hand and stepped behind me slightly.

"Nice to see you remember how to get here," Jimmy called out in his normal jovial tone as we entered the space. He, along with the rest of the band and Hadley, were sitting in the lounge. The mood in the room was somewhat tense but certainly not hostile. I relaxed a bit when Zeke gave me a smile and a nod. It wasn't the warmest of receptions, but at least he didn't look like he'd showed up for a knife fight.

Unlike the sad tableau that was my house, the clubhouse was quite comfortable and stylish in its own way. Zeke's girlfriend at the time we bought the place was an aspiring interior designer. She'd attempted a "swanky seventies vibe," but the place ended up looking like a set from Boogie Nights.

I greeted everyone, then pulled Lucy over to the loveseat by the wall. "Thanks for meeting up on such short notice. Things have been a bit crazy for me lately, but I wanted to get together and get everyone up to speed."

Jimmy was the only one to respond with a simple but upbeat, "Cool."

"Y'all remember Lucy Haddon." I felt the heat creep up the back of my neck as everyone looked at up me blankly. "Of course you do," I said and leaned forward, settling my arms on my knees.

"It's nice to see everyone again," Lucy said a little too cheerily. "My father sends his greetings to all of you."

I had to hold back a laugh. She sounded like a Disney princess welcoming her royal subjects to court. We had the nervous energy of two teenagers coming home after prom night.

I continued, "Um, I know Hadley's let you know a little bit about what's been going on with the tour and everything is great on that front."

Silent nods all around.

"Great, so on a more personal note…"

I had to formulate a careful way to convey the deep feelings I held for Lucy to my band mates while remaining sensitive to their possible reservations about the idea of us having a romantic relationship.

"Fuck it! Okay everybody here's the thing, Lucy and I are together. As in *together*. So… that's… that," I said.

The room remained silent for a few moments longer until Zeke posed a fair but jarring question, "Are you out of your fucking mind, Bam?"

Bam

LUCY LAID HER hand on my back, probably to keep me from losing my shit on my brothers. I glanced back at her and scowled.

"It's a lot for them to take in," she said, talking about them like they weren't in the room.

"I'm okay," I quietly assured her.

"Is that why you stayed in Seattle? So you could hook up with *her*?" Zeke waved a hand at Lucy.

I stood, my body locking in barely controlled anger. "Talk about Lucy like that again and you're gonna have an easier time hitting those high notes."

"Okay, so this meeting's getting off to a bit of a rocky start," Lucy said with a sigh.

Before I knew it, she was on her feet, and her hand was on my chest, feebly attempting to push me back down into my seat.

"Bam, sit down," she continued. I glanced at her and then back at Zeke. He was already on thin ice with me and this made me want to invite him to go skating. "Beau," Lucy snapped, and I focused on her. "Sit down, honey."

I stared down each of my stunned band brothers before slowly lowering myself back on the sofa.

Lucy smiled. "As Bam so eloquently and romantically put it, he and I are in a relationship, we're not just hooking up. I know it's fast, but we've discussed this with my family and my father has given his blessing so to speak. I get that this is way out of bounds, and so does Bam. Believe me, this wasn't planned but it's where we are, and Bam and I are committed to making sure our private lives don't interfere with the upcoming tour." She sat back down next to me and I took her hand.

"Lucy, first of all I'm sorry, I didn't mean to disrespect you. It's just that we've been here before with Bam," Zeke pointed out. "Bam's personal life mixes with his private life and then all our lives are turned upside down. Every interview becomes about him and who he's with. I have to hire security for my parents because the paparazzi are on their property."

I looked at Zeke. "Shit, man, I didn't know that. I'm sorry."

"You're always sorry. I know you're sorry, but here we go again none-the-fucking-less. It's always all about you! The Bam Bam Nelson hour with special guests 'three other assholes from Alabama.' "

"That's bullshit," I spit back. "I work harder than anyone in this band and you know it."

"Of course we know it. You never let us forget it. Tell me; are you really working harder or do you just have to put in overtime to clean up the mess you make everywhere you go?"

"Fuck you!" I rose to my feet again. "When Melody and I were together you didn't seem to have any problem at all with the extra attention. Then, she fucks me over and you get pissed at me? How was it my fault that Melody leaked that video and then cheated on me for the whole world to see?"

"It's not, but you brought that shit into our house." Zeke stood and faced off with me. "Things haven't been the same since, and now you want to do it all over again? Once again, it's all about you and what you want."

"What about Chas?" Jimmy chimed in. "Talk about bringing shit into our house, Zeke. You brought a fucking wolf in!"

"Don't change the subject and stop sticking up for Bam all the time," Zeke snapped.

"I'm not sticking up for him," Jimmy snapped. "I'm just saying he ain't the only one at fault here. Personally I'm sick of everyone's shit...Bam's included."

"You guys are unreal. All I've done for the past seven years has been to help you all. Everything I've ever done is for *this band*!" I shouted.

"That's bullshit and you know it." Zeke looked at me coolly. "Everything you've ever done was to help you run away from home."

Fuck, he was right.

"Okay," Lucy said, standing again. "Let's take a second." She took my hand again and squeezed. "Deep breath. Remember, they love you."

I nodded, releasing her hand so I could drag mine down my face. After a few seconds of tense silence, I turned back to Zeke. "What do you want me to say, man? What am I supposed to do? Turn off the way I feel? I can't. Not with Lucy. You want me to say you're right? Fine, you're right. I've spent my whole life running and I've dragged you along with me. I'm sorry, but I'm done running. I went back home and am trying to put the past behind me for good."

Zeke's face contorted in surprise. "You went back to Elwood?"

"There's a lot to tell, Zeke. I want to tell you about all of it, hell, I want to talk to my friend, but that's the thing, Zeke, I don't know if we're friends anymore."

He dropped his head. "I'm sorry about the money, Bam. I'm so fucking sorry. I swear to you I didn't know what Chas was up to. What I did was wrong, but I promise you I had nothing to do with that other shit."

"I believe you."

"I know Chas is a piece of shit and it's my fault he was here. That's the truth, but can't you see where I was coming from? I needed someone in *my* corner."

"Here's the thing. I *don't* get that," I admitted. "I didn't even know we were in opposite corners. I thought it was us against the world."

"It was, until it wasn't," he said with a certain amount of defeat in his voice. "You say you do most of the work, but I say you took most of the control."

Zeke's words hurt because there was more than an element of truth in them. In an effort to hold onto the family I created, I crushed them. Instead of protecting them, I had become controlling and angry. In an effort to "take the hill" at all costs, I had forgotten to have my buddies' backs, and instead acted like a crazy general marching them to slaughter.

I was so burned out; it hadn't occurred to me that they might all be going through similar things. I figured they were having the time of their lives and I was the only one in pain.

I flopped down next to Lucy again and dropped my face in my hands. Lucy slid her palm along my thigh and her touch instantly soothed me. I raised my head and studied Zeke. "I'm really sorry, brother."

He gave me a quick nod and sat down again.

"So…um…can you guys hug it out and then we can actually have a band meeting?" Hadley asked, and the room busted out laughing.

"Dude, you guys are more drama than my sisters… and they're both actresses," Edward retorted.

"The mute speaks," Jimmy joked, and Edward cracked a semblance of a smile.

"You sure you want to dive into this?" I asked Hadley.

Lucy giggled behind me. I craned my head and raised an eyebrow at her.

"What?" she challenged. "Edward's right. You're also more drama than one Roxie Haddon, and believe me, that's saying something."

I grinned and took her hand, kissing the palm gently, before facing the band again. "So, unless anyone has any objections, Hadley has agreed to be our new manager."

"Fuck!" Jimmy breathed out. "Finally."

Hadley rolled her eyes. "What do you mean, 'finally'?" she challenged.

"It took you a while to accept."

"Two days!" she countered.

He shrugged and gave her a lopsided grin. "Shoulda just said yes right away, I reckon."

I chuckled. "Well, she's said yes now, so shall we move on?"

"Yes, let's move on," Hadley said. "I have something I want to run by you guys."

"Yeah?" I asked.

"Lost Highway found out you guys were in town—"

"How'd that happen?" Jimmy challenged.

"There are a lot of little birdies around," Hadley retorted. "Anyway, they want to know if you want to play next Friday night. Home show kind of thing."

"It's good for me," I said. "You negotiate a good deal?"

"Of course I negotiated a good deal," Hadley said.

I chuckled. "Great. Let us know the details."

The rest of the meeting covered everything from roadie support to travel plans while on the RatHound tour. Lucy and Hadley worked in tandem to fill in the details of what we needed to know, but I had full confidence, the women would take care of everything without any input from us. I loved watching Lucy in her element and couldn't wait to get her home and back in my bed.

* * *

Lucy

Later that night, Bam and I were laying in bed, one more epic love making session under our belts. I had flopped across his chest (my favorite position), and I was tracing his Roses for Anna tattoo while he stroked my back. "So, set up Thursday night, then show on Friday night?"

"That's the plan," Bam said. "Hadley'll have final schedules tomorrow."

"Well, whatever you need me to do, please make sure you put me to work."

"I'm not puttin' you to work, Lucy."

"Um, why not?" I challenged.

"Because you're here to enjoy the show…not work."

"I appreciate that, honey, but if you need help, I want you to feel comfortable asking." I stroked his cheek. "I let Hadley know I was available as well."

"Okay, baby. Thank you."

I smiled. "You're welcome."

"Where's Sully?" he asked. "I haven't seen him all day."

"Dad needed the plane, so he flew it back."

"Wait…Sully's a pilot?"

"Yes." I met his eyes. "Did I forget to mention that?"

He chuckled. "Yeah, baby…you kind of buried the lead."

"He used to fly for United, and he and Dad met at one of the coffee places in…I think Singapore? They kind of hit it off and Sully told him to say hi if they were ever on the same plane. Short story long, Dad offered him a job when the band decided to buy a plane and Sully helped negotiate the sale and guide the refurbishment. He also stepped in as my bodyguard and the rest is history."

"Can I ask a really nosy question?"

I giggled. "Of course."

"How the hell does your dad have so much money? It's not like RatHound's as big as Metallica, you know? I know how much bands make, and the 90s weren't that generous to artists."

"Mom. She's always controlled the money, because Dad's smart and he made sure she was in charge. She negotiated some pretty incredible deals, invested really smartly, and made sure Dad, and the band, kept control over their publishing rights. They never gave up anything when it came to songwriting credits and the like. So, even when the stuff happened with rehab and everything, Mom kept everyone flush, and even gained power of attorney over Jack's finances when Pam died. He went dark for a while there and probably would have lost everything if she hadn't stepped in."

"Wow," he breathed out.

I nodded. "Never ever repeat that."

"I won't." He smiled. "Your mom's a fucking badass."

"You have *no* idea."

"I see where you get that from."

I gave his waist a squeeze. "That's the best compliment on earth."

"Where did your red hair come from?"

"Dad's side. My grandmother looked like Lucille Ball. I got her boobs and hair."

"Shit, baby, your grandmother sounds gorgeous."

"She is…she's just kind of a bitch, unfortunately. Mom makes sure she's managed as well."

"Your mom sounds like she needs a vacation."

I laughed. "She loves *everything* about her life. And she can go anywhere in the world on a moment's notice, so I'm pretty sure she's good."

"What about your brother? Why haven't I met him yet?"

"He's hiding right now." I sighed. "It's annoying."

"Why is he hiding?"

I shrugged. "He does that sometimes. Dad's issues hit him harder than me. I think because he and Dad have always been super close. You know, same sex parent and stuff? He packs up his guitars and disappears for a few weeks every year or so. Dad knows where he goes, but no one else."

"Not even your mom?"

"According to Luke, only Dad knows," I said. "But knowing Mom, she probably made the reservations."

Bam chuckled. "Is your brother any good?"

"At?"

"Guitar."

"Ohmigod, he rivals Robbie. That isn't a surprise, considering Luke pretty much sat at Robbie's feet his whole life, but Luke really is amazing in his own right. A legitimate talent."

"I can't wait to meet him."

"He'll be helping out on the tour." I smiled up at him. "You'll have plenty of time to get sick of him."

Bam rolled me onto my back and kissed me. "If he's anything like you, I doubt I'll get sick of him."

"Give him a week."

Bam laughed, kissing me again, his hand moving to my breast. "I can't seem to get enough of you, Miss Lucy Haddon."

I smiled against his lips and slipped my hands in his hair as he kissed his way down my body. His mouth covered my core and he sucked gently on my clit as he slid two fingers inside of me.

"So fuckin' wet, baby." He kissed his way back up my body, sliding into me.

"Yes!" I drew my knees up higher, wrapping my calves around his back. His mouth covered mine and his tongue slid into my mouth as he wrapped his hand around my breast and squeezed. He rolled the nipple between his fingers as his hips surged into me, his tongue matching the motion with each thrust.

I lost his mouth on mine, but he moved his lips to my throat and I arched my neck to get more. I dropped a leg onto the mattress and mewed as he slid his hand between us and fingered my clit.

"Come baby," he said, his breath coming in pants

as he slammed into me again and again.

I whimpered out, "More, Beau."

He gave me more, pressing in deeper and I exploded around him. He wasn't far behind and he collapsed on top of me, rolling us to our sides to keep our connection. I felt him pulse inside of me for several seconds and I wrapped my leg back around him.

"Wow," I whispered. I stroked his cheek. "You're really good at all this sex stuff."

Bam chuckled. "I'd say you're pretty good, too, baby, but I honestly think even if you weren't, I'd still love it just as much." He kissed my nose. "Because it's different with you."

"It is?"

He nodded. "Everything with you is just… better."

I grinned, dropping my head to his chest. "I feel the same way."

I wanted to tell him I loved him, however, I stopped myself. It was too soon and I didn't want to scare him away, but I'd also never felt this way before.

"You okay?" he asked.

I snuggled closer, kissing his neck. "I'm amazing."

"Good." He stroked my back as he kissed my temple, and I closed my eyes, falling into the abyss of adoration he was providing.

We had almost a week before the hometown show, and I couldn't wait to spend alone time with him on his turf, so to speak.

Bam

THURSDAY NIGHT, THE last of the roadies had cleared out of the theater, which left me and Lucy blissfully alone. We were ready for our show tomorrow, but for now, it was just me and her and I couldn't wait to get her back to my place. I was officially addicted to her body.

She sat, legs crossed on top of a rolling road case used to haul equipment, reading a book. I couldn't make out the title, but she seemed engrossed in it, her finger having woven a lock of her hair around it as she concentrated on the pages. She wore skintight black jeans and a Roses for Anna baseball T-shirt that was tied off at the waist. Her hair was slightly teased and she'd pulled off her high-heeled booties, setting them next to her. She was the perfect picture of good girl, turned rock music video vixen.

"Hey, beautiful, where'd you get that shirt?" I asked through my unstoppable ear to ear grin.

"I know a guy," she retorted coolly, lowering her book.

"Does he know about me? 'Cause I'll kick his ass if he starts to put the moves on my woman."

I slid my hands up the side of her thighs, tugging her toward me, her crotch to my waist. Taking the book, I set it aside as Lucy grinned and crossed her legs around me. I pulled her as tight to me as I could and kissed her deeply and slowly.

"No need to get all ragey—"

"Ragey?" I asked, interrupting her.

She giggled. "Your rage issues are legendary," she teased. "And, should someone 'put the moves' on me, I'll handle it."

"Fair enough. How 'bout we drop this subject and you give me another one of those kisses?"

"What's in it for me, mister?" she challenged.

"Now there you go calling me mister again, you know how I feel about that."

I kissed her again, drawing her closer to my chest. Her soft body pressing against me, making me rock hard. I felt like I might crush her with how tightly I was now holding her. I had to get closer to her. I needed to be *inside* of her...in every way. I needed us to share everything we possibly could with each other. Most of all, I needed her to know how I felt.

"I love you," I rasped. The words tumbled out before I could control myself. Lucy stiffened and pushed, gently away from me. She looked deeply into my eyes, her gaze more intense than I had ever seen. I couldn't breathe. I had never told a woman I loved her, and I was scared shitless.

"I…I…" she quietly stuttered.

Before she could continue I pulled her close and kissed her again. I wanted her to feel how much I burned for her. "Shh, you don't have to say anything."

"It's not that."

"What is it, then?"

She sighed. "It's stupid."

"Why is it stupid?"

"Because I love you," she whispered, her lips barely parted from mine. "I was worried it was so soon, but it's how I feel, so fuck it. I love you. Screw waiting longer to say it."

I could no longer stand it. Kissing would not be enough, words would not be enough. I put my hand under her thighs and lifted her up, and her ankles locked tightly around me. I continued to kiss her hungrily as I carried her to the stack of thick velvet theater curtains that were tucked behind a small storage alcove. I gently placed her down and pulled off my t shirt. She perched on her elbows, arching her back slightly, letting her long red hair fall back onto the crushed velvet. I had to loosen my belt and unzip my pants to relieve the pressure, but before I would undress any more I had to get Lucy out of her clothes first. As I stepped closer to her I could hear her breathing begin to quicken.

I leaned over her and began kissing her neck while untying the knot at the bottom of her shirt. Once untied, I quickly pulled the shirt over her head, but was careful to keep her in the same position. I had full access to her neck and that was exactly what I wanted. She smelled like vanilla and something else…something sweet. More importantly, every time I kissed her neck, she moaned in sweet, short breaths. It was the sexiest thing I'd ever heard. Her body trembled as I cupped her breast. "You cold?"

She shook her head. "Horny."

"I better take care of that, then."

"Hurry," she rasped.

I chuckled and shifted so I could remove the rest of my clothes. Lucy sat up, now wearing only a black bra and jeans. Her current bed of crushed red velvet provided a stark contrast to her beautiful pale skin which seemed to glow in the soft backstage light. Her hair fell down over her lightly freckled shoulders and she stared at me with what I can only describe as "doe eyes." She was adorable and unbelievably sexy.

"You are so beautiful, baby," I said.

"Are we really alone?"

"Yeah," I assured her. "Locked the doors myself."

Lucy nodded, then reached behind her back and unhooked her bra clasp, allowing it slowly slip and fall over her perfect breasts. Fucking perfection.

Lucy licked her lips. "How do you look bigger every time we have sex?"

"Don't worry, I'll be gentle."

"Don't do that, honey. You know how much I hate gentle."

I stretched out next Lucy and kissed her, placing one hand on her ass while the other cupped one of her full breasts. I felt her shudder as her breathing once again began to quicken.

"Breathe baby, just breathe," I whispered, my thumb now working her nipple in slow circles as I continued to kiss her neck. She moaned and I felt her thigh muscles tighten. I moved my hand from her ass and turned my attention to her glorious tits. I greedily took her full C-cups into my hands and began sucking her already hard nipples. I continued to suck and caress while I slid her panties off.

"Someone might come in," Lucy whispered.

"No one's comin' in, baby. I locked up," I reminded her again. "Promise."

"Yo! Bam?" Winston called. "You in here?"

"Shit," I rasped, and Lucy sat up with a start. "Be right there, brother."

"You locked the doors, huh?" she accused as she tugged on her shirt.

"I did, baby…but he's good at lock picking."

"Ohmigod, Bam, seriously?"

I gave her a mild grin and we yanked the rest of our clothes on as quickly as possible. I adjusted my raging hard-on and went to see what the hell Winston wanted…other than to cock block me.

Bam

The next morning, my phone buzzed and I scrambled to answer it before it woke Lucy. I looked at the clock, just after 6:00 a.m. The call was coming from Jaxon Quinn so I quietly got out of bed and answered the call in the next room. "Hey Jaxon, you got news?" I whispered.

"Actually I do, that's why I'm calling or I wouldn't have disturbed you so early."

"Don't worry about it, what's up?" I asked.

"Do you remember when Grady Jones mentioned his lawyer?"

I rubbed my forehead. "Yeah, you asked for his card and he got all shitty with you."

"That's right. Well if you recall his lawyer's name is Harlan Caster."

"And that's significant, why?"

"Harlan Caster is a sleazebag lawyer for the Dixie Mafia. He has also represented Dr. Greene on several malpractice suits, and handled all of Chas' immigration papers. He's a major player in the organization and handles a lot of matters for them."

"Holy shit."

"That's not all, Bam. He was also your father's lawyer."

"What the fuck?" I breathed out.

"I think your mother was killed to send a message."

"A message…to whom?"

"Your father."

My heart raced. "What?"

"Your father owed the mafia a lot of money. He'd lost hundreds of thousands in gambling. In order to work off his debts, he did low level jobs for them whenever asked…until he started refusing. I think they killed your mother to send a message to him and to control him, exactly like they did Dr. Greene and Grady Jones. They paid off Jones and solved Dr. Greene's legal problems, but they had no leverage on your father other than his family."

"That sonofabitch." I swallowed convulsively. "He was responsible for her death and he made me feel like it was somehow my fault."

"If you hadn't left town, they may have come for you next, Bam, who knows?"

"How do you know for certain it was a hit?"

"Dr. Greene's autopsy report was inaccurate in two ways, the time of death and the number of bullet wounds."

"You mentioned those in our interview with him."

"He was instructed to change both of those details," Jaxon explained. "The time of death in order to create an alibi for the actual killer, and the number of shots to conceal his M.O."

"Does that mean you know exactly who the killer is?"

"Yes we do. He's a contract killer often employed within the Dixie Mafia named Arlo Weston, and the bureau has him in custody. That's why I'm calling."

I could barely register the words he was speaking.

"We have your mother's killer. More importantly, we have the people who gave the order. Thanks to Chas' knowledge of the mafia's accounting system and the connections via your mother's case, we've been able to arrest seven high ranking mafia members and dozens of other connected thugs… Bam… Are you there?"

A sound like buzzing bees filled my head. "What? Um… yeah…I'm here."

"Did you hear me? We're going to put a lot of very bad people away thanks to you and your mother."

"Yeah. Thank you…thank you for your call." The phone hit the floor, followed by my knees.

* * *

Lucy

"Bam, honey?" I called as I slipped from the bed and made my way toward the kitchen. I'd barely registered him getting up, but then his voice penetrated my sleep.

I hit the mouth of the hallway just as I heard, "…thank you for your call." Then the clash of something crashing to the floor.

"Bam!" I quickened my steps and watched as his knees hit the floor and his face dropped in his hands. "Ohmigod, baby, what happened?"

I rushed to him and pulled him into my arms.

"Lucy," he rasped, and I cradled him to my chest.

"I'm here, honey. It's okay."

He filled me in on the phone call with Jaxon while I held him on the floor. By the time he was done with the story, I was sobbing and he was comforting me.

Everything this man had gone through made him strong. Probably stronger than he would have wanted to be, but it made him a giant in my eyes and I couldn't have loved him more. I stroked his wet cheeks and smiled through my tears. "You're an incredible man, Beau Nelson. I'm really sorry all those awful things happened, but I'm so glad I know you. I love you."

"I love you too, baby."

He took me back to bed and made love to me with a sweetness and desperation we hadn't experienced before. The rest of the day was my chance to show him people *do* stick around and that I was in it for the long haul. We planned our future together, which included him moving to Seattle and starting a new life with me. It wouldn't happen right away, but it would happen sooner than later, and I couldn't have been more excited.

Tonight though, tonight I got to see my man in his element. Nothing could have made me happier.

* * *

Bam

"Circle of fear!" I yelled, and Winston immediately began clearing the room.

"C'mon y'all, time for the band to get ready! Please exit in a timely and orderly fashion," he hollered cheerfully as he ushered the backstage partygoers out the door. "That's it, ladies and gentlemen, right this way…the show is about to start!"

The circle of fear had been a band tradition from

back in our early club days. No matter where we were playing, no matter how pissed we were at each other, no matter what, the rule was we'd always do the circle of fear. The four of us would gather in a circle, in some quiet place and sing in harmony. The idea was to face each other, quiet ourselves, look one another in the eye and try to get our voices to blend as well as we could before getting on stage. We figured if we could always do this, we could always make great music together. The day we could no longer do the circle of fear was the day we could no longer be a band. This was something we somehow understood as very young men. There is no greatness without intimacy and there is no intimacy without fear.

"Circle of fear gentlemen," I said again as we made our way to the center of the now empty room. "Would you be so kind as to lead us in song, brother Zeke."

"I'd like to sing a song for Anna Nelson," he said smiling.

I nodded and he led us in her favorite Tom Petty song *Wildflowers*.

One at a time, each band member added their voice and we sang to my mother, who I could finally, truly lay to rest. I also sang to a father I could finally begin to let go of.

As we ended our song, we remained facing one another silently until Jimmy smiled and asked, "Anyone feel like pissing off the neighbors?"

"Showtime!" Zeke shouted and we made our way out of the room where Lucy had been waiting in the hallway.

"Hey! There's my woman." I pulled her close and kissed her. I couldn't imagine ever getting tired of kissing her. If I didn't have a show to play right then, I couldn't imagine anything else being able to tear me away from her.

"I could hear you singing through the door," she said smiling.

"You're about to hear a lot more. You gonna be on the side of the stage this time?"

"Maybe, we'll see," she teased.

"We'll see?" I challenged back.

"Oh, I'll be watching, I'm just not gonna tell you from where. I want to keep you guessing."

"I have a feeling you're going to constantly keep me guessing."

"Well, here's one thing you won't have to guess about."

"What's that?"

"How much I love you," she said before pulling me in for another kiss.

"Oh and here's another thing. What I want you to do to me tonight." She pulled me closer and whispered specifics in my ear.

"Miss Haddon!" I stood up straight. "That's downright filthy! Does your father know you speak like that?"

"I have a pretty good idea." I turned around quickly to see Rex Haddon standing in front me, Roxie by his side.

"Holy shit!" I blurted out.

"Nice to see you too, Bam." He smiled wide and

gave me a hug. "We just wanted to come by and say have a great show." He moved his attention to Lucy and the others as they began walking to the stage area. I stood there still somewhat stunned.

"You coming, silly?" Lucy asked, holding out her hand.

"You go on, I'll see you out there," I said smiling.

She disappeared through the darkness of the curtains and I could see my band mates at the side of the stage waiting for the house announcer's cue. Usually I'd be pacing, or obsessively adjusting my in-ear monitors, counting down every tick before I could get to my drum throne, but right now I just wanted to stay in this quiet darkness for a moment longer.

I thought about the broken road that had brought me here and about the broken man I had been when Lucy found me. She saved me from myself, helped heal me with her love, and most importantly, showed me the way home.

Lucy

Five months later…

I STUDIED THE ice skating rink that now sat on my finger. Four carats of oval diamond perfection in white gold, a diamond wedding band nestled close to it.

"Hey, you gonna keep staring at that, or do I get some of your attention?" Bam complained.

I sighed and rolled my head to meet his eyes. We were currently on the plane heading to Scotland for our honeymoon.

If you'd told me six months ago that I'd fall instantly in love with this man, I'd have hit you. Rushing head first into relationships had never been my thing…but when it came to Bam, that all went out the window.

"I can't believe you picked the most glorious, ridiculously over the top rings for me," I said.

"Your mom helped, baby," he admitted. "I paid for them, just to be clear."

I giggled. He'd proposed to me with a candy ring pop, blue raspberry (my favorite), and since he didn't drive a fancy car or live in a big home, I didn't press him for a lavish ring. I told him to surprise me, and man, did he.

Mom had insisted he and I sit down and openly discuss our finances in order to make a plan for the future, and knock me over with a feather, I discovered my man liked to save money. Or as he liked to put it, "What the fuck do I have to spend money on?"

He'd surprised me on our wedding day when he'd settled the huge rock on my finger, then the diamond band next to it, which is where I discovered that I was who he had to spend money on now.

"Did you read the inscription?"

"What? No," I squeaked. "I haven't taken it off since you put it on my finger."

"Read it," he ordered.

I slid the diamond band off my finger and held it to the light…which is when I burst into tears. "Oh, Beau."

The inscription simply said, "Home."

He leaned over and kissed me. "You're my home, baby."

"Back atya," I whispered. "Now, read yours."

He slid his off his finger and laughed.

I'd inscribed, "Love always, Bambi."

We were excited to be starting our lives together and even more excited for the all-expenses paid honeymoon to Scotland…a wedding gift from Kade Gunnach and his family.

But more than anything, I was most excited to be going on tour with my husband, rather than my boyfriend.

I may have given Bam a home, but he'd given me something far more precious…his heart.

New York Times & USA Today Bestselling Author Piper Davenport writes from a place of passion and intrigue, combining elements of romance and suspense with strong modern-day heroes and heroines. She currently resides in the Pacific Northwest with her author husband, Jack Davenport, and an obnoxious YorkiePoo named Pepper who may or may not be an international spy.

Like Piper's FB page and get to know her!
(www.facebook.com/piperdavenport)

USA Today Bestselling Author Jack Davenport is a true romantic at heart, but he has a rebel's soul. His writing is passionate, energetic, and often fueled by his true life, fiery romance with author wife, Piper Davenport. Twenty-five years as a professional musician lends a unique perspective into the world of rock stars, while his outlaw upbringing gives an authenticity to his MC series.

Like Jack's FB page and get to know him!
https://www.facebook.com/JackDavenportAuthor

www.ingramcontent.com/pod-product-compliance
Lightning Source LLC
Chambersburg PA
CBHW060356310726
48976CB00003B/848